About the author

After a career in teaching Nick Morrice took early retirement and is now pursuing a second career as a writer.

Other titles:

Discovered in Kathmandu - How I found my Nepalese family
The Lily and the Rose
I, Franz Schubert
Cycling with Cuthbert
The Ballad of the Magic Chalice

www.nickmorrice.co.uk

THE CASTAWAYS

Nick Morrice

THE CASTAWAYS

Vanguard Press

VANGUARD PAPERBACK

A CIP catalogue record for this title is available from the British Library.

ISBN 978 1 784654 95 5

Vanguard Press is an imprint of
Pegasus Elliot MacKenzie Publishers Ltd.
www.pegasuspublishers.com

First Published in 2018

Vanguard Press
Sheraton House Castle Park
Cambridge England

Printed & Bound in Great Britain

For Adie

Native American Ten Commandments

1. The Earth is our Mother. Care for her.
2. Honour all your relations.
3. Open your heart and soul to the Great Spirit.
4. All life is sacred. Treat all beings with respect.
5. Take from the earth what is needed and nothing more.
6. Do what needs to be done for the good of all.
7. Give constant thanks to the Great Spirit for each new day.
8. Speak the truth: but only of the good in others.
9. Follow the rhythms of Nature: rise and retire with the sun.
10. Enjoy life's journey but leave no tracks.

1
A Tricky Confrontation

'Risk all, dare all', had been Clive Thompson's watchwords all his working life, and apart from one or two spectacular failures, they had served him well. So now, as he approached his final year as form-master to the top form at Hengistbury Hall (boarding school for boys and girls, aged 7–13), he decided he would go out with a barnstormer of an idea. Over the next three terms they would pursue a theme in literature, art and music, of islands of castaways and fantasy adventures. Gradually he would feed into the mind of the headmaster, Dr Crabb, that the annual leavers trip might take place on a remote tropical island – a daring idea, but a possible one if approached carefully and intelligently. Dr Crabb had founded the school fifteen years ago, with the express notion of offering a curriculum which would transcend the limitations of current-day preoccupations with examination results. He felt strongly that school life should offer more than a purely academic regime. True, he had run foul of the system at times, and had had some awkward brushes with the authorities during his tenure. But he had always got away with it, because the school exam results were good if not spectacular, and the children were mostly happy, well-mannered and enthusiastic. His abiding principle (which of course he expected his staff to adhere to) was: teach properly and methodically, and the examinations will take care of themselves; always keep in mind a broader picture, for this alone will be memorable and inspiring.

When Mr Thompson entered the classroom on the first day of the Autumn Term, his class of eight boys and eight girls fell silent and stood up politely at their desks. They exchanged 'Good Mornings', everyone sat down and then enjoyed a short chat about the summer holidays. The usual preamble about timetables and various mundane announcements followed, and then Mr Thompson launched into his theme.

“Apart from preparing you for your Common Entrance and Scholarship exams later this year, which we will take as a matter of course, my plan is to follow an island theme. There are several books to read, starting with *The Swiss Family Robinson* by J. D. Wyss, written in 1812 (a bit long and tedious so we will only be dipping into it); *Treasure Island* by Robert Louis Stevenson; *Swallows and Amazons* by Arthur Ransome written in 1930; and William Golding's *Lord of the Flies,* written in the post-war years. There is also an interesting short story called *The Man who Loved Islands* by D. H. Lawrence, and a piece of music by Debussy called *L'isle Joyeuse.* We will look at poetry about islands, and study paintings of islands. You will also be writing your own poems, and doing your own paintings. And of course, we shall study, and later perform, Shakespeare's *The Tempest* as the leavers' play."

"Then can we go and live on a desert island, sir?" asked Christian, always the devil's advocate despite his name.

Much to everyone's surprise and delight, Mr Thompson replied, "My idea exactly, Christian. We are of one mind, for a change."

"Where will we go, sir?" asked Karen. "How about the Seychelles?" and she exchanged a snigger with Victoria who sat next to her.

"I haven't worked out the details yet, Karen, but that is a possibility. Or the Caribbean maybe? or the South Seas?"

A few gasps and excited murmurings: the year's project was launched.

***

Fast-forward nine months to the occasion when Dr Crabb was in his study facing the redoubtable Mrs Seymour. She had always been one of the most difficult parents to deal with, and on the sensitive issue of this year's leavers' trip he knew she would be particularly troublesome. Maybe a little alcohol would soften her up.

"Sherry, Mrs Seymour?" he asked, as he walked over to the drinks cabinet.

"No, thank you – much too early in the day for me."

Oh dear, an unpromising start. Better not pour one for myself in case she gets the wrong impression. So he sat down opposite her on his favourite armchair, where he felt at his most relaxed, and said, “So, where shall we start? Your letter said you had some issues you wanted to discuss.”

“Three, to be precise.”

“I had hoped we had covered all the details at the recent parents' meeting,” he replied, knowing it was a forlorn hope.

“The obvious details, yes, but a lot remained unsaid, as I am sure you are aware. Hidden, and covered up.”

Dr Crabb looked bemused. “Hidden and covered up? Surely Mr and Mrs Thompson brought everything out into the open, and there was a full and frank discussion.”

“They have worked out the children's meals, I will grant you, and most of the Health and Safety aspects have been considered. Even so, there is a lot which is still being left to chance, in my opinion.”

“We can't cover every *single* eventuality, Mrs Seymour. As you know, Hengistbury Hall prides itself on offering an adventurous educational experience. It is one which...”

“I know, I know,” Mrs Seymour interrupted. “You never cease to advertise the fact. I am amazed that some of your school's more hare-brained schemes haven't run foul of Her Majesty's School Inspectors. But that is not the issue here. What concerns me are the deeper, more psychological issues which none of the parents dared mention last week even though everyone knew that they were simmering below the surface.”

"Such as what? Please explain, Mrs Seymour, because what concerns you I am sure will concern others as well."

"The first is the matter of sex, Dr Crabb. I know you are a single man, but even you must be dimly aware of its lurking menace."

"The matter is all in hand," said Dr Crabb, calmly and soothingly.

"All in hand? What do you mean, all in hand?" Mrs Seymour retorted furiously.

Dr Crabb felt beads of sweat breaking out on his forehead but was determined to maintain his composure. "We are fully aware of the problem. Although the children are only just entering their teenage years, we know (how shall I put it?) that change is afoot," he said with a smile, but Mrs Seymour only scowled all the more. He cleared his throat and went on, "Matron has spoken to the girls about the matter. From the way she reported back to me, the girls appear to be much better informed on the subject than she is. They will be two to a tent, after all, and they are sensible girls. I am sure you have nothing to be concerned about on this matter."

"But what about the boys, Dr Crabb? Have you addressed this issue with them?"

Dr Crabb decided to sit up and be more assertive – he was not going to be intimidated by Mrs Seymour a moment longer. "I have spoken to the boys, along with young Mr Crawford, their History teacher, of whom they are all terrified. We have made it absolutely clear that there is to be no misconduct of any kind. The boys have all taken a solemn pledge on this matter, and the consequences of breaking that pledge will be extremely severe, I can assure you. I honestly believe you can rest easy, Mrs Seymour." He paused to draw breath.

"Well, I hope so. At least you appear to have realised that there is a possible problem. Let's hope they don't go wild once they have been let off the leash. And this brings me to my second point."

Dr Crabb inwardly groaned, but assumed an air of patience and docility. "Do carry on, Mrs Seymour."

"As you know, they have all been subjected to a host of literature pertaining to life on desert islands and suchlike over the last nine months – some of very dubious quality, I might add, but I will leave that aside, for the moment. I want to refer to that horrible book, *Lord of the Flies,* which caused so much upset in the class, at least among the more sensitive ones."

"I am also aware of that, Mrs Seymour. But I am going to defend Mr Thompson here, because whatever the merits or demerits of the book, it did serve the purpose of highlighting how appallingly young people can behave towards each other if left to their own devices."

"But that is just what you are planning to do, Dr Crabb: leave these children to their own devices."

"Well, yes, up to a point we are – I will admit that – but under carefully controlled and planned arrangements. The difference is that they have been *prepared*, whereas the boys in *Lord of the Flies* were not. And of course they are not going to be totally abandoned on an island, but will be visited each day with supplies, and Christian will have a mobile phone in case of emergencies – so it is quite a different situation, you must agree. As far as that book is concerned, Mr Thompson has been leading classroom discussions and I have sat in on these, and they were extremely positive and constructive. The book, as you probably know, describes in vivid detail the worst excesses of children's behaviour, and one of the challenges Mr Thompson's class faces is how to restrain their wilder impulses and behave with respect and kindness towards each other. The importance of the Golden Rule of behaviour, 'Treat people the way you'd like to be treated', has been stressed time and again in our preparations, and I truly believe the children have taken this on board."

"Well, let's hope you are right, Dr Crabb. The consequences of failure would probably result in the closing down of your school, so on your head be it. Finally, there is the matter of the 'Hearties' and the 'Swats'. Everybody knows that the Upper Sixth this year is a very divided class, and these unfortunate terms have been in common parlance all year. You know what I mean: 'he's a swat', 'she's a hearty' and so on. I am really worried that this is going to cause problems when the children are left on their own. I am not saying there is any antagonism between the two groups at the moment, but I can see how, to put it simply, the big toughies will simply squash and run rings round the smaller ones."

"I know exactly what you are talking about, Mrs Seymour. Half of the class veers more towards sport and so-called 'heartiness', while the other half are more studious and 'swatty', as they call it. But again let me try and reassure you. Do you remember the production of *Hiawatha* the form put on last Christmas? They really worked as a team, and there was no sense of division: each one brought his or her own quality to the production, and I strongly believe they will do that again on this trip. And because of *Hiawatha* they have adopted the Ten Native American Commandments as their Code of Conduct – much better than trying to preach to them, or moralise. Who knows, this trip might even have the effect of making them a more united group. Basically, they are sensible, responsible children, wouldn't you agree, Mrs Seymour?"

"Well, I have to agree that they have been a reasonably civilised, well-behaved class of children – but they are only children. Let's hope castaway life doesn't go to their heads. At least it is only for one week."

"Barely even a week: a day getting there, and a day coming home, so they will only be having five days and nights entirely on their own. And a member of staff will be visiting them each day, remember. Have faith, Mrs Seymour. All will be well, I am sure, and it will be an adventure which they will remember for the rest of their lives."

2
Introductions

The parents had insisted on an educational purpose for the trip. To this end, Mr Thompson asked each pupil to decide on a personal project, for which a special item could be included in their luggage. (They might have a 'secret' wish as well, but that's up to them.)

"Hello, I am Alice, the smallest in the class and without doubt the swattiest. I am short, with curly hair, and wear thick glasses. Some of the Hearties barely know I exist, and they certainly don't talk to me but that suits me fine. I am very self-absorbed and like to keep myself to myself. I think a lot, and work comes very easily to me so I have been known to help out a Hearty if they get stuck. I get on well with the other Swats, and my best friend is Becky. My project is to study beetles, bugs, insects and spiders (at a safe distance, of course) because I love little creatures like that. Charles Darwin was an ancestor of mine, so it must be in the genes. My special item is a large black dustbin bag full of stage costumes because – and this is my secret wish, except it isn't a secret – I want to put on a play of *Alice in Wonderland.* I know the other Swats will enjoy doing this because they all like acting. They all know who they are going to be, and I think it will be fun."

"Hello, my name's Becky, and I am short like Alice with long black hair which I like flinging from side to side. I laugh a lot, and am lively and happy. I am going to be a great writer when I am older because I can't stop writing stories, and my secret wish as a castaway is to write my first novel. My special object, or objects – cheating a bit – are a microscope and a magnifying glass because I am going to study pond-life. And if there aren't any ponds, then stream-life; something like that, anyway. I am hoping to see lots of exotic dragonflies!"

"Hi, I am Christian, and the Form Captain: tall, dark-haired and quite good-looking – sorry if that sounds a bit vain. I am going to be in charge of this trip which is a lot of pressure but I guess I have a sort of authority which the others respect. I am a laid back, calm sort of guy. Basically my project, if you can call it that, is to see the week runs smoothly, and write the Official Log. My special item is a surfboard. I am told there will be some good breakers there, and one of my life's ambitions is to tour the world surfing all the top beaches. This will be a perfect opportunity to improve my technique. (Secretly, I want to patch up my relationship with Olivia. It's been going badly recently – my fault more than hers, probably – so I'm hoping this week will smooth things over.)"

"I'm Corey, and I am sports-mad. They say I am tall and gangly, with fair hair and always on the move. I'm not that bright in class, but I'm fun and sociable. My special thing is a football (and a pump, of course). If I hadn't been able to bring a football I think I should have gone mad. My project is to organise games and sports, certainly plenty of running and jumping events – maybe even make some javelins and discuses. Could end up with a sort of Olympic Games, who knows? I am good at organising things and people and I'm just looking forward to a great week on our island. (My secret? To get Karen to take some notice of me. She must know I adore her, but she can be really standoffish and it drives me mad. Maybe she'll at least start talking to me by the end of the week.)"

"Hello. I am David, the class nerd. I am very average to look at, with glasses, dark hair and average height – just ordinary. I am bookish, clever and interested in everything under the sun, except for sport which I find tedious in the extreme. Fortunately I have a good sense of humour, and a tough skin, so I can put up with any funny remark made at my expense – it's like water off a duck's back! I got in quickly with my project which is to make a film of our week. So my special item is the school video cam with plenty of batteries, and I am really looking forward to using it. (Now you are going to think this is really weird, but my secret ambition is to find out if there are any spirits on our island, like Ariel in *The Tempest*. I believe in that sort of thing – nerdish, eh?)"

“Graham the layabout they usually call me, but I don't care. It's a pretty fair description because I do like just loafing around, laughing at everyone who takes life seriously and has 'projects' – how I hate that word! I am average height, fair-haired, always relaxed and laughing. But there is one thing I take seriously, and that's my 'cello. I play well and plan to do it professionally, so I will have to bring it along for my daily practice. I will take some manuscript paper because I hope to do some composing; hopefully I will be inspired by a week of sea and sunshine – sounds cool! I said I will try and make some percussion instruments as well, but God knows how. That's about it: just looking forward to a great week, swimming, sunbathing, all that stuff. Secrets? I would like to try and make a frisbee, because I couldn't bring it as I brought my 'cello.”

“Hi, I am Helen, and I'm just looking forward to being with my friends on a sandy beach with palm trees, and a warm sea to play around in. I am quite tall for my age with a fair complexion and long straight blonde hair, which I hope won't get too messed up because I normally wash it every day. I have brought my flute along as my special thing, because I think it will be nice to play as I walk along the beach. What I would like to do, if possible, is to make some reed pipes, or panpipes, out of bamboo. I have looked up how to do it, and I think it might be possible. Anyway, I have brought a good knife and some string, so that's my project.

(My only worry is not having enough to eat, because I always seem to be hungry. I am not telling anyone about this because it makes me sound greedy, but they wouldn't let us starve, would they?)"

"My name is Karen, and I have enjoyed reading about islands and castaways this year. I am average height, with longish brownish hair, and I am not especially bright but that doesn't bother me, because I am really sporty which I think is far better. My project is botany, and I will be taking a flower-press and a proper flower-book to bring them home in. I am looking forward to swimming and playing volleyball on the beach, and I know Lucy is bringing one. (I will try to explain my secret but it's really complicated: you see, my best friend is Victoria, but unfortunately, we both like Zak. I think Zak likes her more than me, but then I think Corey likes me, but I am not sure if I like him. I just hope something gets sorted out.)"

"Hi, I am Lucy. I am fairly tall with quite wavy brown hair, and always try to keep a straight back and walk properly (which might seem an odd thing to say but it's important to me). I want to be a doctor when I am older so I am going to be the nurse in case anyone falls ill, or gets bitten, or anything like that. I have been on a First Aid course, and both Mum and Dad are doctors, so we have talked about it a lot, and I'm really looking forward to it. I hate this thing about Swats and Hearties – it's so silly, and anyway I am neither one or the other. My project is reptiles and mammals as I am sure there will be lots of lizards and snakes, frogs and toads, all that sort of thing. Bye! Oh, and yes, I will bring a volleyball."

"Hello. I am Maia, and my best friend is Lucy who I just love because she is a great example to me, and I really look up to her. I am a bit too thin probably, but I have this absolute dread of getting fat. I have long wavy pale brown hair, and a palish complexion, and I love painting watercolours. My dad is a really good artist, and he has taught me lots, so I am just going to paint and paint. It's going to be fabulous. I am neither a Swat nor a Hearty, because I get on pretty well with everyone. They are my friends, and I am really looking forward to spending time with them without any adults. Bliss! (If I have a secret wish, everyone knows it already because I love designing new clothes, so I am going to design some beachwear. I want to have my own brand when I am older.)"

"Hi. I am Oliver, and my project is to make a map of the island. I won't have any of the right equipment apart from some binoculars so there will be a lot of guesswork, but I reckon I will be able to make a good stab at it, just by walking around and pacing out. Anyway, I love maps. Oh yes, I am short and stocky, with lots of energy and enthusiasm. My luxury is to take the brilliant kite I was given for my birthday, and fly it over the ocean and from the tops of hills. (Secretly, I have some instructions from my dad who is a film producer.

He in interested in making a film there so I will be writing notes on good locations.)"

"Well, I am Olivia, and I am amazed my mother ever let me come on this trip, because she has been such a fuss-pot about everything. I mean, really, it's not as though we are going to die, is it? I am tall with long straight black hair. My worst thing is that I can moan a bit, and get moody. My project is fish because I love snorkelling, so I said that as long as I could bring a snorkel and flippers (and not lend them to a soul), I would do a project on fish. My idea of heaven! I love swimming and diving, and have done it for years, so I will be in my element. I am definitely not a Swat, by the way. (The only snag is that Christian's here, and he's been such a pain recently. He'd better be really nice to me, or else...)"

"I'm Philip, and my special thing is a pair of binoculars because I am mad about birds, and that's my project: ornithology. I am obsessed with parrots so I'm really excited because the island should have lots of them. I am shortish, but stocky and strong, with brown hair which sticks up. (I do have a secret thing I want to do as well, but I am not saying it here, because it will give the game away. I will need to sneak in my small tool kit, but I am also keeping quiet about that.) I am more of a Swat than a Hearty, I suppose, but I really love sport too, so where does that leave me? Who cares anyway!"

"My name's Tom: short, black hair, ears which stick out – that's me – and I am going to make daily reports on the weather. I have been allowed to bring all the equipment needed to record air pressure, temperature, wind speeds, rainfall and so on. If David is Nerd Number One, then I am Nerd Number Two, because I am nutty about weather and clouds. I will be climbing up trees with my telescope (that's my luxury) and scanning the horizon for signs of approaching tropical storms which of course I hope we will get. A typhoon would be my idea of heaven! My secret is to climb as many trees as possible as I am not allowed to do that at home, and to make a boomerang."

"Hello, I am Victoria, and I am going to do sketches of butterflies because there should be some lovely ones there. So my special item is a butterfly net. I would have preferred to take photos of them, but we are not allowed our phones which is a real drag, but I suppose I can see the point as there won't be any electricity to charge them. I am medium-height, with medium-length, medium-brown hair, red lips and cheeks, and blue eyes. (I am a bit crazy about Zak, but sometimes he never even seems to notice me as he's always singing and stuff, so what can I do? And I can't discuss it with Karen, even though we are best friends, because she is crazy about him too. It's all a bit tricky.)"

"I'm Zak, and I am tall with blonde hair, a toothy smile, and tanned skin because my parents take me abroad a lot. I am not bright at all, but I am happy, which is all that counts. And I am a folk-music freak so I am never too far from my guitar (which is my luxury, of course), and I make up songs and stuff. I had to think up a project which was guitar-based, so I said I will write poems and songs inspired by our castaway life – not exactly calypso, but my own style of music. I am a cool creative kind of guy, and will just wait for the vibes to strike and then get composing. Should be dreamy. (Girls are my big weakness, I suppose, and I can see a few troubles ahead, but hey, it'll be okay, I reckon.)

3
Blissful Arrival

Day One
Captain's Log

Our first steps on our desert island, with its palm-fringed, wave-washed, unspoilt sandy beach, were very special: the sun was beating down, a gentle breeze was blowing across the sand and rustling through the leaves and our feet were sinking luxuriously into warm soft sand. It was a sort of "Aaaah..." moment. I reckon we'd all experienced something like that in the past when we'd been taken to beaches in England, or on the continent, but we knew at once that this place was different. It was so primitive, somehow: you could still imagine the early explorers paddling here in their huge double-hulled outrigger canoes (we'd been told about these at school before we came), pulling up on the sandy beach and being as entranced as we were on their first day. And this reminds me that there is a place called First Landing on Fiji, I think it is. Well, I bet this scene isn't much different and hasn't changed much since then, roughly a thousand years ago, give or take the odd hundred.

Unfortunately, this blissful moment didn't last long because Mr and Mrs Thompson and Mr and Mrs Crawford set us to work almost immediately.

We knew this was going to happen, so we had to be patient and put up with being ordered around, until they were completely satisfied that everything was properly organised for the week.

They had brought along spades to dig loos, mallets for the tents, bins and bin bags for refuse and recycling; we had to forage for firewood, and we had to organise the cooking arrangements. We had been told to bring a tent to share with our partners, clothes, towel, washbag, mosquito nets – well, all the things that you would expect to bring. We'd been given a list which included stuff like plate, cup, cutlery, torch, matches, medical things, mosquito spray etc. All the usual things. I am not going to write down all the boring details, or even describe the first day's preparation except to say that it seemed to go on forever, when all we wanted to do was to jump in the sea. But in the end it was worthwhile, and as Leader I needed to know what all the arrangements were, so this is how things stood by the middle of the afternoon.

Between the beach and the sand dunes there is the largest tent which contains all the kitchen stuff. In front of this is the cooking/eating area.

On one side were the four girls' tents: Alice and Becky, Maia and Lucy, Olivia and Helen, Karen and Victoria. On the other side the boys' tents: David and Philip, Oliver and Tom, me and Corey, Graham and Zak. No great surprises there.

The whole point of this week is that we will be living simply, so there will be no frills, just the essentials. Every day, either the Thompsons or the Crawfords will come by the little local ferry from the nearest town on the main island with supplies. (I ought to explain at this point that most of our parents have flown with us to the main island, because they also fancy a week's holiday in the sun, but they are strictly not allowed to come and visit us!) I will meet them with a couple of others at the jetty, where we will collect the food for the day and discuss anything which needs to be discussed. If everything is okay, then we will be left in peace. That is the only communication with the outside world we'll have for a week, apart from the one mobile phone in case of emergencies. What can possibly go wrong?

Before the adults left, everyone else handed in their mobiles, and I will be given a freshly charged one each day, just in case. I was also left with a small axe, a couple of spades and a big sharp knife, which should be useful for coconuts, at any rate. We were of course extremely grateful for everything they'd done, but equally it was wonderful to see the back of them. At last we were on our own. It was mid-afternoon and the sun was still high in the sky when we took our first plunge. Ecstasy! A lovely warm sea, with big rollers but nothing so huge as to be frightening. We just played and played for as long as we wanted, and then flopped on the warm sand for our first sunbathe. Everyone had been told to bring towels, sunhat and sunblock, and we were pretty careful about the sun because it was mighty hot, I can tell you.

"I wanna be here forever!" sang Zak – his first bit of singing of the week.

I called an assembly later on as there were a few things to say. “First, we will take it in turns to do the meals and washing up, so this evening it will be Becky and Alice. Tomorrow morning, I will be on with Corey, then lunch will be David and Graham and we will carry on like that, alphabetically. That way nobody should forget. There won't be much to do as it will all be cold: fresh fruit, bread, cheese, salad, milk, honey. Well, you all know that anyway, so don't expect anything special – plus anything else we might find around the island, such as bananas, coconuts, papaya and so on.

“The next thing is that in the mornings you must do something on your project. You can spend all day on them if you want, but certainly in the mornings. They don't have to be exclusively yours; you can get help from others if you want, that's pretty obvious.

“There aren't any rules as such, but we will get together at nine a.m. every morning after breakfast and say the Commandments, because that's what we promised to do.

“If there are any problems, come and see me, and if you are feeling ill, go and see Lucy. In the evenings, after supper, we will build a fire and Zak will lead us in singing songs. Any questions?”

There weren't any, so everyone drifted off for the next couple of hours to collect more firewood and we found plenty on the edge of the beach. Some people went into the woods a bit further inland, and came back with stacks, so wood clearly isn't going to be a problem. This went on until we had a good pile. Then we had supper. I watched to see that this went well before I had mine, and am pleased to say that everyone was patient and nobody barged in or anything. There seems to be a good atmosphere, and really we just thank our lucky stars that we have finally made it, after all the months of planning and meetings with parents, and travel arrangements and all that stuff. Sometimes it seemed as though the whole idea was going to be kiboshed, because some parent thought of yet another snag, so there had to be another meeting to discuss that. What a drag! Anyway, we are here now, and it's going to be great.

After supper, we went down to the water's edge and watched the sunset. Maia did a painting, David filmed it, and it was spectacular, unlike anything we had ever seen before: just an amazing spread of colours, blues, yellows and reds, and the orange ball of the sun gradually sinking into the ocean, then dipping below the horizon. Indescribable, really. It didn't last long, and soon all the reds and yellows drained out the sky, and it turned greyish – but while it lasted it was truly awesome – and there are six more to come! It started to get a bit cold so we went back and lit the fire. Soon there was a cheerful blaze, and we sang songs. We sang that old favourite *Oh Island in the Sun* but I expect by tomorrow Zak will have something new for us. With Graham on 'cello and Helen on flute the music was great. We should have a few percussion instruments by tomorrow evening as well, hopefully.

I am writing this in my tent under our little Tilley lamp, and I am pretty tired now. I think I have covered everything. The real fun will start tomorrow. Corey is already asleep, and snoring, but he's told me to poke him if he snores, so I will.

***

"Graham, listen to this:

Hmm, hmm, hmm,
We've left a land behind, so far away,
Alohawa, alohawa,
And now we've reached your sunny shores.
Touch us with your special magic,
Let your sunlight shine though our hair
And through our souls
Alohawa, alohawa.

"What do you think?"

"Great, man. Keep going. I'm drifting off to sleep."

***

"What do you think so far, Becky?" asked Alice once they had done all the necessaries, and were lying in their sleeping bags.

"Wonderful! I never really ever believed it would happen, did you?"

"No. But there's something funny about this place, isn't there? Have you noticed anything?"

"Yes, I have. I feel as though we are being watched."

"So do I. A bit spooky, but okay. Quite benevolent really."

Becky laughed. "Another big word! Where did that one come from, Alice?"

"Latin. It means kindly, from *bene* meaning 'well' and *volens* meaning 'wishing'."

"A wishing well! Oh, I wonder if there is one."

***

"Corey?"

"Hmm? Was I snoring?"

"Yes."

"Sorry."

"Was I okay?"

"How do you mean?"

"Well, you know: not too bossy."

"No, you were fine. Someone has to say things like that, you know, keep us a bit organised, and we're used to you."

"Okay. Tell me if I go too far, won't you?"

"Don't worry, I will. Now shut up, as I'm asleep."

***

"I think you've just got to tell him."

"What?"

"That he's getting too big for his boots."

"Do you think it will make any difference?"

"Well, it's worth a try."

"Okay. The thing is, Helen, I do love him, but he just seems to ignore me when he's in one of his

'I'm in charge' moods. He gets all arrogant, and takes command, and seems to forget I even exist."

"You just need to tell him, Olivia."

"I'm no good at confrontations, you know that. I s'pose you couldn't do it for me, could you? As my best friend?"

"Could do. I'll try and catch him when he's off guard."

"Thanks, Helen."

"That's okay."

***

"What are you reading?"

"*The Time Machine*. And you?"

"*Hitchhiker's Guide to the Galaxy*."

"Are you planning to learn it by heart?"

Philip hit him with his pillow.

"Ow!"

"Serves you right. Anyway, you seem to read nothing but time-travel books nowadays. What are you planning – a great escape?"

"Possibly. I'm just researching the subject at the moment, and when I get home there will be a new book waiting for me called *The History of Time-Travel* which has just come out. Books are all very well but I want to experience it for myself one day."

"Shall we make a film about time-travel?"

"Yes, let's."

"Shall we make a time-machine ourselves?"

"Yes, let's."

Philip hits him again.

"Ow!"

***

"Victoria?"

"Hmm?"

"What's your best thing about being here?"

"Being away from my brother."

"I was going to say exactly the same thing!"

"Actually we've been getting along better recently. But it's when he teases me that I hate him. At least I have managed to get him to knock on my door now and not just barge into my room."

"What I hate about Andrew – well, not hate exactly – is when he is rude to Mum, or at least doesn't say thank you, or starts whining when she complains about him leaving all his clothes on the floor, that sort of thing."

"Let's forget about them now, and enjoy a week off. It's going to be so lovely here - can't wait till tomorrow."

"Me too. G'night."

"G'night."

***

Tom and Oliver were lying on their backs with their heads poking out of the front of the tent – they were looking up at the night sky, the brightest array of twinkling stars they had ever seen in their lives.

"Wow!" was their only whispered comment.

After a few minutes of silent amazement, Oliver whispered, "Are we in heaven, Achilles?"

"I believe we are, Patroclus."

A few more moments passed, then, “Time?”
“Time.”

***

Maia and Lucy were the only ones still up. They had crept down to the water's edge, and were dancing very slowly in a close embrace in the shallows. Their feet stirred up little bubbles – catching the light of the moon, they twinkled then popped gently as they burst. They were humming the evening's campfire song, swaying from side to side, cheek to cheek. Maia kissed Lucy very softly on her neck... After a few minutes, they were running back, giggling, across the soft sand to their tent. What bliss!

4
Unusual Experiences

Day Two

Alice had found a few beetles under the palm trees; she built a little pen to put them in, and then she was able to watch and observe them. “I know I'm funny,” she said to herself, “but this is what I like doing.” Then she made some detailed drawings which she was pleased with, before letting them go. “Tomorrow I will focus on spiders – to be handled with care, of course.”

By mid-morning she'd had enough of being cooped up under the darkness of trees, so she sauntered out into the light and onto the beach. For a few minutes she watched Corey as he worked: chopping, shaping and binding bits of wood which presumably he had dragged out of the forest. “Looks fun,” she thought. “I wonder what he's doing exactly?”

The only time she remembered speaking to him was last term when he needed some help with a quadratic equation. She coughed a little as she approached him over the warm sand. He looked up. “Hello, Alice. What are you doing?”

“Not much, really. I can't do anything till the others get back.”

"What others?"

"Becky, Maia, Lucy, Tom, Philip, Oliver and David."

"What's going on with them?"

"We are going to rehearse a play I've written."

"What's it called?"

"Alice in Wonderland."

"Oh."

"We'll probably start this afternoon."

"I see."

There was a long pause while Corey continued to sharpen a long stick with his knife.

"What are you doing?" asked Alice.

"Making javelins. Want to help?" he asked, looking up.

"Okay. What can I do?"

"You can take over from me while I go and look for two others like these."

He showed her what to do, and how to be careful not to cut herself. There was one stick lying on the sand at his feet.

"You can start on that when you have finished, if you like. Try to keep it roughly the same length as the other one, if you can."

He jogged off back up the beach, as Alice got down to work. In the distance she could hear Graham playing on his 'cello. Back at school she thought it the most ridiculous thing that anyone should bring a 'cello to a South Sea island – crazy! – but now she felt it was not such a stupid idea after all. Unaccompanied 'cello, with wave obligato, quite nice, really.

***

Becky was pleased with her progress. She had been walking for about an hour up the coast looking for a pond ("but *pond* sounds so English," she thought) when eventually, after searching inland beyond the mangroves, she found what she believed was called a 'coastal pond'. Presumably it was fed and washed each day by the incoming tide. She had been happily searching along its fringes for a while, when she heard footsteps nearby. It was Tom wearing a curious hat with corks hanging from the brim, making him look more nerdish than ever, in her opinion.

"Hi, Tom."

"Hi, Becky. How's it going?"

"Look," she said holding up a jam jar. Inside were a few small crustaceans, shrimps and suchlike, which she had gathered from the water's edge with a small net.

"They're cool," said Tom. "What are you going to do with them?"

"I am going to sketch them, then return them to the water. Oh, look!"

Across the water a sapphire-blue dragonfly was darting from place to place.

"That's the first I've seen!" and she immediately took up her sketch book to make a quick drawing. "And that..." as another one came into view, "is a damselfly. You can tell because it is smaller, and holds its wings lower over its body. Oh, this is amazing, Tom! I hardly dared hope I would see them here! Aren't they beautiful!"

"Have fun!" said Tom, resuming his walk round the island. Already he had taken some barometric readings, and had made notes about air temperature alongside the times of day. He had also been up in the middle of the night to take more readings – leaving Oliver snoring gently, he had crept out to take another look at the stars. A light breeze had picked up, and the temperature had fallen quite a bit. He took more readings by torch light and wrote them all down when he was safely back in his sleeping bag. By the end of the week he would have a full record of climate and weather on their desert island. It would be his first step on the road to becoming a meteorologist!

***

It wasn't exactly a mountain, but a good-sized hill. Once Oliver had scrambled his way through the patches of woodland that fringed the island, not without a few scratches, the vegetation decreased as he made his ascent. Of course there were no pathways, but even so it was quite easy going. The palm trees and coconut trees had given way to a more open rolling grassland. There was little that could be described as useful vegetation – small scrubby bushes were the most common feature. Underfoot the way was hard, stony and dusty, but this was far easier than trying to beat a path through forest or jungle. Furthermore, he could see where he was going, and the hilltop only looked to be about half an hour's walk away.

He was hoping that the summit would give him a panoramic view of the island. This would be a good starting point for his map. He had to rely on counting his paces to get some idea of measurements, and every so often he would stop and make a note of how far he had walked.

As he pressed on up the slope, he gradually became aware of a strange sound. It was as though a flock of birds had swooped close over his head – later he described it as a fluttering of wings, which quickly came and went. Of course he had looked up at once but there were no birds to be seen. He certainly hadn't imagined the noise, so what could it have been? Still puzzled, he carried on. He reckoned he was well over halfway so decided to press on to the top. By now he was having to take continual swigs from his water bottle as the sun was beating down. He had decided not to look back at the view until he was right at the top, but he never made it. The more he climbed, only pausing occasionally to look up, the more he realised he was no longer getting any higher. It was most peculiar. He glanced at his watch: eleven-thirty already! Everyone had promised to be back by midday for roll-call and lunch. He realised that he would have to give up for today and return the way he had come.

He sat down for a moment and rewarded himself with the view. It was magnificent: he could see their beach, with its fringe of palm trees, the sand and sea beyond, and the long curling breakers. Spectacular! David must come here and do some filming. Perhaps he would solve today's little mysteries as well. “They're right up his street,” he thought.

He added up all the paces he had taken so far, and did a quick sketch of the view in front of him; it seemed to make sense. Already he could give a sort of shape to the western side of the island. As soon as he finished, he set off quickly down the mountain.

***

Victoria and Karen had decided to set off together. After all, where there were wild flowers, there would also probably be butterflies. But really there was only one thing on their minds: Zak. Normally he would be the last subject they would discuss, but somehow things were a bit different here, and they felt more free to say what was on their minds. Karen spoke first. “Have you talked to him since getting here?”

“Not really, only to say 'hi' and stuff. Oh, and we played a bit in the waves yesterday afternoon. He is so funny!”

“About the same with me. He grabbed my hand as we raced down the beach as well. I adored that!”

“Let's be honest: we both love him and there it is.”

“Hmm, I guess you are right. So what's to be done about it?”

“Nothing, I guess. Just have to live with it.”

Victoria took Karen's hand, and said, “We won't let it spoil our friendship, will we?”

“Of course not, Vicky! I don't s'pose we're the only girls to like Zak, he's probably got dozens of girlfriends outside school. He's just a really cool guy, and lots of fun, and nice-looking, too.”

“You're probably right. So what are we to him, anyway? Oh look, my first butterfly!”

A large yellow swallowtail had settled down on a bush covered in pink and white flowers to their right. They had arrived in one of the lushest parts of the island, where a waterfall fed into a pool which was surrounded by blossoming trees and bushes. The girls quickly got out their sketchbooks, glad to be diverted onto a different subject. They fell silent, enjoying the peace and harmony of the place.

“You know, it's funny,” said Victoria, “it's almost as if she, or he, wants to be drawn. Look, Karen, do you see, he's just preening himself, showing off his wings. In England you wouldn't get a moment before they're darting off.”

“Perhaps he knows you need a bit more time because you haven't got a camera.”

“Don't be ridiculous!”

***

Philip had brought a *Guide to the Birds of the South Sea Islands*, and was pleased with his first sightings. The collared lory parrot was the only one he had definitely been able to identify, he'd checked it carefully to be absolutely sure:

The male has bright scarlet cheeks, throat, breast, and upper abdomen. The crown is dark purple. The nape is lime green and red and some of the feathers on the nape are elongated. The wings, back, and tail are greenish. The lower abdomen is purple. The bill is yellow-orange, the feet pink-orange, and the irises are orange-red.

That was definitely the lory – brilliant! He had first become aware of it from its high-pitched shriek. He followed the sound and eventually saw the bird high up in the forest canopy. It was far more exotic than any bird he had ever seen in the wild at home, so he kept very still, watching it for several minutes, before it shot off deep into the forest.

Now to make a start on his secret plan.

***

Olivia had never experienced anything like it. Ever since her parents had taken her to the Maldives and she had learnt to snorkel, it had remained her favourite thing to do. But if the tropical fish there were wonderful for their variety of colours, shapes and sizes, the sea-life here excelled all her expectations. And, for the first time ever, she was swimming with turtles! It was quite amazing. She had always been called a 'Water-baby' because ever since she was tiny, she had loved being dipped in the sea by her dad. It made her squeal with laughter, so they knew early on that she would never be afraid of water. Olivia quickly learnt to swim, had taken to diving, and simply never looked back; and for her final year at prep school she had been captain of swimming. The school team beat all the local schools in swimming and diving matches, and Olivia had even secretly thought of herself as a future Olympian.

But for now she was happy to relax in these beautiful warm waters, and enjoy the underwater world off the coast of her tropical island. “I will record everything, and see how many varieties I can identify. Thank goodness I brought a decent guidebook with me! This is so heavenly. I can't understand why everyone doesn't do it!”

***

Further along the beach, Christian was having similar, but above-water, thoughts. The rollers were magnificent and although he was fairly new to the game, he knew that after a week his balance would improve, and he would begin to 'read' the waves better. It was all a matter of timing, and coordination. He recalled some of the basics which he had read last night:

You should lie on the board so that the nose is only a few inches above the water. If you lie too far back on the board and the nose is way up in the air, your board won't plane across the surface and you’ll be pushing against the water. On the other hand, if you’re too far forward and the nose is under the water, you won’t go anywhere and you’ll probably just end up falling off! Most beginners make the mistake of being too far back on their board.

Well, that had been fairly simple. Paddling also was pretty straightforward, but the next step, which was basically just lying down, would be harder work.

Once you've got yourself lying at the right spot on your board, the next step is to arch your back a bit so your weight is on the bottom of your rib cage. Your feet should be together and lifted out of the water so they don't drag. This position is HARD for the very new because of the muscles involved. You're going to get tired quickly, but you'll soon build up the necessary muscles.

Okay, working on that. Now, what was next?

The arm stroke itself should be deep. Don't "lily-dip!" As you paddle more, you'll build up your muscles.

Okay, more muscle-toning. Where are you, Olivia?

Once you're good at pushing the board for momentum in the whitewater, you can start to try and paddle to gain momentum. As the whitewater comes towards you, climb on the board and start paddling towards shore. Once the whitewater catches you, grab the rails and hang on!

Right, let's give it a go... hang on, I've missed out a step here, what came before that? Oh well, here I go – oh no!... aaaaah!... missed it!... where am I?... where's my board? (tumbling around beneath the waves, straining for the surface, gasping for air).

What a disaster!... hope no one's watching... not quite got it yet... never mind, try again.

***

"Well, I am not going to be short of bamboos!" thought Helen. "There must be zillions here!"

Fortunately she would not have to cut any down because there were stacks just lying at her feet, and they were nicely dried out so making it easier for her to cut into their brittle stems.

She had her handy step-by-step guide which she had practically learnt by heart, and also the very few additional items such as ruler, sandpaper, wax, needle and thread she needed. She decided to concentrate on steps 1 and 2:

Step 1 Select lengths of dry, mature bamboo. Inside diameters may vary, but 5/8 inch is a good size. Use a craft knife to strip away any surface detritus. Cut the joints off either end of the lengths. Use a stick or piece of metal slightly smaller than the bamboo's interior diameter to gently drill out the pith.

Step 2 Cut the lengths to within 1/2 inch of the recommended length for each note. Lengths for a five-pipe set could be as follows: 'C' at 6 1/16 inches, 'D' at 5 3/8 inches, 'E' at 4 3/4 inches, 'G' at 3 15/16 inches and 'A' at 3 7/16 inches.

Okay, let's get started.

There was a rustle of leaves as a slight breeze picked up. She was sitting on the ground in a clearing, surrounded by tall bamboo stems reaching up to the sky. She never realised they could grow so thick and vast. The wind blew over the leafy tops, creating a strange harmony of music. Helen felt enveloped in a natural world of sound, not mournful exactly, but unusual and mysterious, and the canes clattered gently together, providing a percussion accompaniment.

***

Graham had made a start on a new composition for 'cello, flute, guitar, panpipes and percussion. Now he needed to make some percussion instruments, but how do you begin?

"How do you make a drum, for heaven's sake?" he said out loud.

"Easy," said a voice behind him.

He turned and it was Becky, who was walking back to the beach with a few jam jars full of pondweed, as far as he could see.

"Go on then, show me."

They had never had much to do with each other, but maybe she'd be willing to help him. She was a good deal brighter than he was, he knew that.

"The first thing is coconuts," said Becky. "We drink the milk, cut out the flesh for lunch, then you have two empty shells to hit together. Easy!"

"Why didn't I think of that?"

"After that, we'll make a drum. I know an easy way to do that, too. Come on, let's go and get started."

***

Lucy and Maia were going to help each other: while looking for wildlife they would find painting subjects at the same time. To be honest, as long as they were together, they didn't mind too much about their projects. They had never had an opportunity before to spend so much time in each other's company, so they were going to make the very most of it. They would walk and talk, and if anything turned up, fine; if it didn't, well, never mind.

After about half an hour's walking inland, they came to a grove of coconut palms so they settled themselves down and simply listened and looked. This required a lot of patience but there was oodles of time, and for once they had no timetable to follow and no one to come and tell them that they must go and do something else. They became very quiet, trying to make themselves invisible, hoping that what they were looking for would simply come to them. It took time, but gradually the light and shadows created by the trees and undergrowth began to form a picture in Maia's imagination, and tiny rustlings revealed a lizard and a frog for Lucy to observe and draw. With no consciousness of time they immersed themselves in the scene around them, and remained very quiet, sketching and painting.

***

The most unexpected meeting was Zak and David. Who would ever have thought these two would have much to say to each other? David was heading out for his morning's filming, came across Zak and decided that music would make a good start. Zak was working on a new song, gradually feeling his way into the lyrics and the chord sequences, when he became aware of the whirring behind him. Looking up, he saw that he was being filmed, so he launched into a massive improvisation. He was so pleased with his spontaneous outburst of song that later he wrote it all down, intending to teach everyone that evening over the camp fire.

"How do you do it? Where do you start?" asked David, when the song and the filming had come to an end. "I just wouldn't know how to begin."

"Well, it's like this, see: you just have to open yourself to wherever you are, and whatever you're feeling, trust your instincts and then the song will simply flow out of you. It's all a matter of letting go, without any thinking, just let it happen, kind of thing. You know what I mean?"

"Not really," said David, laughing. "I don't work like that. I am a thinking kind of person, and I like to know where I'm going. I work it out beforehand and make a plan and then I start."

"Hmm, I'm not like that, you see. I really don't like knowing where I am going. It's like if I write a story at school. I just kind of start it, and see where it takes me. I know that's not how we're s'posed to do it, but I find that's the only way it works for me. Then it's like the story simply writes itself."

So they had quite a lot to talk about after all.

5
An Island of Mystery

Everyone was back at camp at midday; there had been no mishaps, no accidents, so Christian let everyone go for a swim apart from David and Graham whose turn it was to prepare the food. He had been concerned about some of the Swats (he was going to drop that word from his vocabulary from now on, it was so stupid) going off by themselves, but he clearly needn't have worried. For the rest of the day they would probably stick around together much more, and if anyone wanted to go off by themselves, they would have to tell him where they were going and make sure to be back by five p.m. He really didn't anticipate any trouble.

After lunch, Alice and her cast told him that they were going to start their rehearsals, but they would only be going up to the far end of the beach and wouldn't be out of sight, so that was fine. The musicians, Zak, Graham and Helen would spend the afternoon together, Corey and Christian would work on a sports programme for later in the day when it would be cooler, which left Victoria, Karen and Olivia to talk about their boy-problems. So everyone was occupied.

Captain's Log

I don't know if there is a particular way in which a Captain's Log should be written, but I am not a Captain and there is no ship so I am just going to do it my own way. There is lots to report and I only hope I don't leave anything out.

Everyone got back early so we swam at about four p.m., and then played beach volleyball, thanks to Lucy who had brought the ball, and Corey who had helped her put up the net. It was fantastic fun, but we got so hot that we all had to have another swim. Really, we are having a great time!

After our meal (which included coconut milk and coconut, courtesy of Becky and Graham), we lit the fire and had a sing-song. Zak announced his new *Island Anthem* as he called it, so he sang it through, telling us to join in as we picked it up. The finished version went roughly as follows:

Boys (refrain):
Ba ba ba ba ba ba
Ba... ba... (continue while girls sing verse)
Girls: *Island of our dreams*
friend of our soul
you are one with us, you are one with us
in sleep and in waking
in memory, in forgetting
you are home for us, you are home for us.
Girls (refrain):
La la la la la la
La... la... (continue while boys sing)
Boys: *Radiant sunshine*
sparkling waves

vibrating with light, vibrating with light
a place of magic
and heavenly bliss
We've found our home, a home of delight!

Nearly everyone had something to hit or play or bang together for percussion. It was really cool! Helen hasn't quite got her panpipes together yet, but otherwise we had guitar, flute, 'cello, and four coconut shells. Hopefully there will also be a drum by tomorrow. Becky has said we must all look out for gourds tomorrow, and she has explained what these are. You cover them with a skin – where will that come from? – and then hey presto, you have a drum.

The sound we made with our singing and our funny mixture of instruments was quite extraordinary, and David filmed it, so everyone back home will see and hear the music we are making. Philip suggested we could make a CD, and we all think that's a great idea, so we will have a competition for the best name of our group. We can't have 'The Sixteen' because that's already taken – anyway it's a bit boring. 'The Beach Kids' and 'Castaway Crooners' are the best so far, but there's still room for improvement, I reckon.

I then asked everyone to say what had been going on for them, and this is really when a whole lot came out which I hadn't been aware of, but when you added up all the bits together, it made for a pretty strange day, weird and wonderful. In order to cover everything, I will begin with the morning.

We first heard from Oliver who told us about his strange experience going up the mountain. He told us about a peculiar fluttering sound, then about how he didn't seem to be getting anywhere; he just could not get to the top of the hill. Something prompted him to look at his watch, and he hared back down the hill.

This prompted Tom to report a similar incident when he was also losing track of time. He had been scrambling towards the south-west tip of the island, where it's all rocky and craggy, and was enjoying the waves splashing against the rocks when he also heard the same sort of fluttering noise. He said it was quite different from the wind, a bit like a flock of seagulls flying very close over his head. He suddenly thought of the time, and realised he would be late if he didn't turn back straight away.

I then asked if there had been any other surprises this morning, and Alice spoke first. "The best and most interesting thing this morning was making javelins with Corey. It was really fun."

We were all a bit gobsmacked at this, but Corey said, "Yeah, it was great! Alice and I were a cool team!"

Then Becky spoke up, "I had a good time with Graham making percussion instruments. Well, at least, we made a start."

Again, we looked at each other with some surprise, but Graham said in his usual laid-back manner, "I had no idea what to do, but Becky came along and got me started, so it will be okay now, I guess, with her help."

So now we went on to the rest of the day, and this is where it all became really interesting. I asked Alice how the play rehearsal went, and at first she was a bit hesitant, which is very unlike her, but then Philip or somebody nudged her so she started to tell us. "To start with, we went into the forest because it was so hot on the beach. We walked on until we found a kind of clearing and we decided this would be all right for rehearsing our play. So we got going and it all started very well but after about ten or fifteen minutes we heard something very odd. Now I don't really believe in any of these things, but while we were rehearsing we kept having to stop and say, 'What was that?' because there was like a very high twittering noise, almost like a giggle, coming from above us in the trees. There was nothing there of course, but it was very strange."

David interrupted at this point. "I had my video cam with me, so I filmed where the noise was coming from, but nothing has come out, as far as I can see. But it was definitely there, and I mean to find out what it is!"

I asked if anyone else had had a strange experience. And nearly everyone had something to say. First there was Corey who spoke up for me as well, because I had been with him all afternoon.

"You know those javelins we made. Well, they just wouldn't fly! I know they weren't great but they should have flown a bit, but they just plummeted straight to earth as soon as we let go of them. Now I didn't hear any flutterings, or gigglings, but I was aware of something else and that was like a deep booming noise, quite soft, and it wasn't coming from the sea, but from the forest behind us. Just every so often. And it usually came when the javelin flopped down to the ground. Isn't that right, Christian?"

"Yeah, that's about right."

The other things were tiny but still a bit odd. Tom's weather equipment is behaving oddly so he says, and Becky who normally can't stop writing stories is suffering from writer's block, and as soon as Karen tries to do anything with her flowers, she has to struggle with strong gusts of wind blowing them away, and this afternoon my surfboard kept twisting round and sending me under the waves – all very odd. On the other hand, Helen had a funny, but nice feeling when she was making panpipes, as if there was a kind of music in the air; Olivia and Karen and Victoria have all had a good cry, and feel much better for it and Zak is amazed at how he has never written so much in his life and the words and tunes are just pouring out of him.

Otherwise everything is going well: nobody is ill, or wants to go home, or has come to see me about any issues so I was able to tell Mr and Mrs Thompson when they arrived that everything was fine. I did say that Tom thought there was a storm brewing, but he would say that, wouldn't he? Anyway, we have waterproofs and stuff, so I reckon we will cope, but the sky looks as clear as clear to me.

End of day's log.

***

"Lucy."

"Yes?"

"Do you think there is something funny about this place?"

"I think it's possible, but it doesn't really worry me. What is important is that we all keep our heads, and don't go mad or anything. I think those commandments are really important. As long as we observe those, we will be all right. The Native Americans believed in spirits of places, but so did all sorts of people, like the Egyptians and the ancient Greeks, and I expect there are spirits of streams and waterfalls – why not? I am sure they are quite harmless as long as we respect their territory. Don't you agree?"

"You're so good, Lucy! You're like a sort of mother to everyone. I do love you!"

"Can we go to sleep now?"

"Hmm, let's."

***

"The next thing is to get some coloured leaves, and somehow attach them to the frame." Philip was showing David how far he had progressed.

"Are you going to make a complete outfit?"

"If I have time, yes. It will be my memento of our trip."

"I think it could be our symbol, or a logo."

"We'll see what the others think when it's finished."

***

Victoria and Karen had been focusing on flowers, one doing botanical drawings, the other pressing petals, identifying and making notes. It was a bit frustrating at times because of the gusty wind, but in the end they had made some progress, and were of course enjoying working together. With Karen's book, they had identified the very common frangipani with its five-petalled white flower and yellow centre, a yellow beach hibiscus, huge spreading bushes of purple morning glory or ipomeia, and the yellow-green flowers of the liriodendron or tulip tree.

"Don't you think we're lucky to be here?"

"Of course I do. It's a beautiful place, and we're with our friends, so what could be better?"

"Do you think the other stuff, you know, about Zak and Corey, will get sorted out?"

"I think it will, but I'm not sure how."

"I think so, too. But we're having fun, aren't we?"

"Sure are. Night night."

"Night night."

***

Tom wanted to observe the conditions down at the sea shore, so he and Oliver were taking a late evening stroll. It was much warmer than the previous night, so they were only wearing t-shirts and shorts. It was also uncannily calm, and Tom feared the worst. They stood at the water's edge, their arms loosely draped over each other's shoulders. The sky was inky black apart from a few streaks of light which the full moon reflected onto the distant clouds hanging over the horizon.

Tom explained to Oliver: “Sometimes, the weather changes suddenly just before a storm lets loose. You become aware of a weird calm and quiet before a storm hits, even though it is still warm.”

“What happens exactly?”

“A change in the atmosphere as a storm builds up. Storm clouds pull in warm, moist air from all around and a storm system develops. The air travels up through the clouds and then shoots right out over the top of the cloud, and then back down again. On the way down, the air becomes warmer and drier. So it might *seem* to be very stable - but then all of a sudden a thunderstorm breaks out, without warning.”

“Hmm. So is that what you think's happening now?”

“Quite possibly, one can never be sure. (Pause, then he glanced across.) Ready?”

“Ready.”

“Race you back?”

“Sure!”

***

“I am sure he will come round soon,” said Helen consolingly. “He can't possibly ignore you all week.”

“But he's not even looking at me,” sobbed Olivia. “What have I done wrong?”

"Nothing. I really believe he is just a bit nervous, and doesn't know quite what to say. I'm sorry but I haven't been able to catch him on his own today but I will tomorrow. Try not to worry. This is a nice place, our island, and I'm sure everything will work out."

"Okay. Thanks, Helen. Honestly, I think I would go mad if I didn't have you to talk to. What about you? How are you feeling about everything?"

"I just think we need to listen and watch. I don't know exactly what's going on, but basically I think the island is on our side, even if that's a bit of a funny thing to say. C'mon, let's sleep well."

"Sure."

***

"What've you enjoyed most today, Alice?"

"Swimming and volleyball."

"Me, too. Oh, and finding coconuts."

"Why do you think you haven't been able to write a story?"

"I've been thinking about that, and the only conclusion I can come to is that I am meant to be writing the story of us – in other words, a true story for a change, because all my other stories have been made up. But really I don't need to make one up here, because it is all so unusual, I mean this place and what's going on here, that I will simply write this story, our story, and call it 'The Castaways'."

"Hmm, that sounds a good idea. I think somebody needs to write it down, and you are the best writer in the class."

"I'm going to talk to all the people who are doing drawings and paintings, because I think that we can get it published when it's finished, with all their illustrations."

"David can promote it with his film."

"Brilliant! And then we can make a proper film about it!"

"And do it all over again!"

"How amazing that would be!"

***

"So what do you think, Corey?"

"What do you mean?"

"About this place – spooky, or what?"

"I dunno. We've only been here a day, for Chrissakes! I expect there's some simple explanation for it all – anyway, David's here and he'll find out what's going on, if anyone does. Leave it to him, I reckon."

"Guess you're right. So what are you going to do tomorrow?"

"I am going to try and make some hurdles. I just have this idea about hurdling down the beach. It would look so cool, and David could film it. Better than *Chariots of Fire*! Actually it was Alice's idea to make hurdles. I think she enjoyed helping me more than doing her project, drawing beetles or whatever it was, which sounds pretty boring. So we'll probably work together again. And you?"

"I've got those waves to conquer. I know I can do it, but for some reason I was totally out of balance today; dunno what it was... except I do. Trouble is, Olivia's still on my mind, and that means I haven't been concentrating properly. I really must talk to her... but I just don't know where to start."

"Just start!"

"Hmm, easy for you to say that."

"No, honestly, I mean it. Just go up to her and be nice'n'friendly, and smile your big smile, and it will be fine. I bet you anything."

"Okay, mate, I'll give it a go. You're probably right."

"Course I am, mate!"

***

Graham and Zak were on a roll, improvising duets on 'cello and guitar as they sat under the palm trees behind the tent area. They filled the night air with strange 'island music' as they liked to call it. They had prepared and practised for this before the trip by watching YouTube videos of music for the same combination of instruments, and had tried out a few improvisations, experimenting with different but closely associated key signatures, until they began to create a pleasing blend of sounds. The idea was to play Nocturnes which would gently caress everyone to sleep, like lullabies. The music was slow and relaxing, dreamy, one might say, and the combination of the plucked guitar and the bowed 'cello worked well.

The music drifted across the sand, and into the tents of the Castaways, lulling them towards restful sleep, while the island responded in its own mysterious way, ever-watchful, listening.

6
A Storm and a Rehearsal

Day Three

When the storm broke, it was as violent as it was sudden. The rain had started at about six a.m., just as the early risers were beginning to wake up. Tom knew what it meant so he quickly went round to tell everyone to stay put in their tents, and not be tempted to get up and look. "The best thing is to stay under canvas, keep dry and keep hold of your tents. There is no knowing how long it may last, but not losing your tents is the main priority, so stay in them, then they won't get blown away. It is going to get mighty windy!"

He was right. You could feel the wind tugging at the guy ropes and the canvas, trying to rip it out of the ground and hurl it up into the sky. It was as much as they could do to keep themselves weighted down and grounded, to prevent themselves becoming airborne. The noise seemed to be as loud as a jet aircraft so they couldn't have made each other heard, even if they had tried. Occasionally there was a thud, as the branch of a palm tree landed on the sand nearby, and coconuts regularly hit the tents, causing occasional shocks as well as slightly nervous laughter.

Tom measured the wind speed at about 45 mph at its highest, so he soon realised that it was not going to reach hurricane status and it might even blow itself out by the end of the morning. Maybe it was hitting the main island to the north harder, but if this was as strong as it was going to get, then they should be reasonably safe.

By positioning himself carefully between the tent flaps, David captured some footage of branches and swirls of sand being tossed chaotically across the beach. A coconut landing dangerously close by made him withdraw his head like a tortoise into the tent. But at least he would have some filmed record of the storm.

***

Lying low for three hours had become tedious – and they were soon suffering hunger pangs for breakfast – but gradually the storm lost its energy and started to dissipate. By about eleven a.m. it seemed safe to emerge from under canvas and view the scene: it was a mess, but not a scene of total destruction or devastation such as they had seen on their TV screens back home, with images of buildings destroyed and cars tossed around. It was more as though the beach had had a very thorough wash, clean and brush-up. It had left a trail of debris, certainly, but the landscape had probably withstood far worse forces of destruction before so it was nothing out of the ordinary. If this was the worst that could happen, then there was not too much to worry about for the rest of the week.

The kitchen tent was in chaos because there had been no one to hold it down. Several pots and pans had been blown around the beach, as well as litter from upturned dustbins. Christian organised some clearing up while the breakfast crew and a couple of others secured the tent and put together a meal from the scattered remains of yesterday's supplies. At least there would be plenty of bananas and coconuts today, thanks to the high wind. By midday, order was more or less restored, and everyone had something to eat and drink. The sun was streaming down again, and once the meal was cleared away, there was no morning left to pursue projects, as such, so the rest of the afternoon was deemed to be free time, with a roll call to be taken at four p.m.

The castaways broke up into groups: the players to rehearse their play; Graham to help Helen with her panpipes; Zak, Corey, Victoria and Karen to go for a walk, and see where that took them; which left Christian with Olivia.

They had been sitting far apart but when they were left alone they were forced to acknowledge each other's presence.

“Hi,” they said to each other, then Christian took the initiative, and walked over to Olivia.

“Come on, let's be friendly. I'm sorry I haven't been, and Helen spoke to me over breakfast, and so, well, can we make a fresh start? I mean, well, you know...” he stumbled.

Olivia looked up at him, and said, “What's been going on with you?”

“I think I've just been under a lot of pressure, having to take charge of this trip, and really it's made me worried and anxious... so I guess I just became forgetful about you. I'm really sorry, Olivia, I mean it, and now... well, I just hope you can understand.”

“Yes, I do, but it would've been much easier if you'd just spoken to me about all your worries, instead of bottling them up, and keeping your distance. You know, we're friends, and I might've been able to help.”

“Yeah, I know. I've been really stupid.”

“Well, that's okay. C'mon, let's see what's happening, shall we?”

So they sauntered off hand in hand feeling a great sense of relief.

***

The spirits (or whatever they were) were still abroad – the storm hadn't blown them away – and as soon as the play rehearsal began, they seemed to be up to their tricks. Or at least so it appeared to Alice, who was of course the last to believe in these things, but there was enough going wrong to make even her wonder if the play wasn't being jinxed.

She had cast it as follows:

Alice.....................Alice
White Rabbit........Oliver
Duchess..............David

Caterpillar............Becky
Footman..............Lucy
Cheshire Cat........Tom
Mad Hatter...........Philip
March Hare...........Maia
Dormouse............Becky
Queen of Hearts...Oliver
King of Hearts.......Philip

They had moved their rehearsal to a more inviting location, near the waterfall which had been discovered by Karen and Victoria the day before. There was lush grass to walk on, and hummingbirds were feeding on the frangipani blossom which grew in abundance here, so it was altogether more appealing. It might even serve as their performance space at the end of the week. Oliver pointed out that the audience could sit on the boulders which fringed the water's edge. They agreed with this. Then Maia recommended that the stage could be the reasonably level patch of ground which had frangipani as an attractive backdrop; the woodland behind could be used for exits and entrances, and there were tree stumps and a fallen trunk which would be natural stage props. It seemed ideal really, so with that in mind, they began.

Alice falling down the rabbit hole presented a slight challenge until David remarked:

"Suppose the opening scene when Alice is reading takes place halfway up that tree. The rabbit can come along that branch, and climb down the tree, Alice can follow him, as if down the rabbit hole, and she can say her lines about what it feels like to be falling as she's climbing down the tree."

This seemed to make sense, so Alice and Oliver climbed up the tree, tried out David's suggestion and it seemed to work pretty well. They knew they would have to improvise because *Alice in Wonderland* was somewhat alien to this terrain, and adapting to their tropical surroundings was part of the fun.

"What happens next is that Alice's tears turn into a vast pool of water," said Alice, "so here Becky (as the mouse) and I can start swimming around. In fact, you can all join in because the book says that a duck and a dodo and a lory - whatever a lory is (to which Philip chimed in: "A lory is a parrot, and it is actually a native here") – so now we know – and an eaglet and all sorts of other curious creatures had all fallen into the water as well, so we can all have a nice cooling swim in the water, while I have my conversation with the mouse."

So the next part of the rehearsal was very enjoyable: while Alice tried to engage the mouse in conversation, not very successfully because she thought the mouse did not understand English, then thought that it was a French mouse that had come over with William the Conqueror, so tried to speak to it in French, but on saying "Où est ma chatte?" the mouse gave a sudden leap out of the water, and Alice said hastily: "Oh, I beg your pardon! I quite forgot you didn't like cats," at which the mouse replied in perfectly good English, in a shrill and passionate voice (this was Becky's first line): “Not like cats! Would *you* like cats if you were me?”

All this went on amidst a lot of screaming, shouting and splashing around from the other members of the cast. All in all, it was a very bizarre scene to be taking place in the middle of a tropical forest, and reduced the entire cast to helpless laughter.

Once they had dried off, sunbathed for a bit and generally calmed down, the rehearsal resumed and this is where it started to become interesting, making Alice begin to suspect a *less* than benevolent presence lurking in their sylvan setting. The tree stump which Becky sat on as the caterpillar started making her twist and twitch around, as though she had a bad itch. The itching grew worse until eventually she leapt off with a great yelp: ants! She ran yelping into the trees where she could strip off. Lucy hurried after her; armed with her First Aid kit, she applied various lotions until Becky was in a more comfortable state.

“I am *not* sitting on that stump again for anyone,” she firmly announced when she came back. “Madam Producer, you will have to find me a less ant-ridden prop.”

Ants in a tree stump might of course have a perfectly natural explanation but not the rolling around of a tree trunk which must have lain on the forest floor, totally still and inert for many years. They used this as the table for the Mad Hatter's Tea Party, but as soon as Philip, Maia and Becky sat astride it, the trunk began to shift and wobble around as though it thoroughly resented being woken up from its long sleep, and was determined to shrug them off. Eventually it calmed down, and they were able to make a start but it had been a curious moment. Surely an old dead tree trunk can't have a mind and will of its own?

"No, of course not," affirmed the rationalist David (who, despite his interest in the spirit world, was at heart a sceptic), and Alice totally agreed with him.

"Take no notice," she said. "It was nothing to be concerned about."

"But you weren't sitting on it," said Maia. "It definitely moved of its own accord, just as we came to sit on it. Wouldn't you say, Philip and Becky?"

"I would say so," said Philip, and Becky nodded her head in agreement.

"Well, have it your own way," said Alice, "but until I see or feel something with my own eyes, I am not going to be convinced."

They rehearsed the tea party without any further problem. Alice wanted to practise one more scene before the afternoon was over, and this involved Tom as the Cheshire Cat. For this he would need to find a sturdy branch of an overhanging tree which he could creep along safely, and peer down at Alice, covering himself with a leafy bough from time to time to give the semblance of appearing and disappearing, as it does in the book, while they have their conversation.

This started well enough. Tom had found a thick branch, and Alice was standing below him, looking up. But what Alice hadn't realised is that she was standing on a particularly boggy bit of ground, and while her attention was totally on trying to remember her lines, while staring up and talking to Tom, she did not notice that she was gradually beginning to sink. It was only when she began to feel mud and water creeping round her ankles and feet, that she realised she couldn't move. However hard she tried, she was firmly stuck in a muddy oozy patch of soggy wet ground, and her legs just would not budge. “Help! Help, someone! Can't you see? I'm stuck!” she cried out.

For a moment everyone just smiled a bit at her predicament, and a few mean thoughts like “serves her right” ran through their minds. But then they all hurried to free her, which of course did not take too long. Alice was furious at the indignity of it all. The rehearsal came to a premature end, and while the others ran whistling back to the beach, Becky helped Alice regain her composure as well as her muddy shoes and socks.

“There, you'll be fine,” said Becky, but Alice scowled and said nothing.

7
Magic in the Air

Karen, Victoria, Zak and Corey had a rough time trying to find a path through a particularly dense part of the forest, where there obviously was no path. The boys went ahead with sticks, beating down the undergrowth as best as they could, and the girls held their arms over their heads, to prevent being scratched by the long straggly creepers and vines which kept twisting around in the air, slapping into their faces.

They were getting a bit tired of this when an exclamation of "Wow!" came from up ahead. It was Corey. "The worst is over, guys. There's a clearing in the forest – really beautiful – and there's a pool, a bit overgrown with weed and stuff, but it's really nice."

In a moment they were all breathing comfortably again. Although it was still dense forest, rays of sunlight filtered through the leaves above, casting a strange dappled effect across the water, which was overhung by white, heavily-scented blossom. Its fragrance filled the clearing with a sweet, heady atmosphere, quite overpowering the four young people.

"What's that tree, Karen?" asked Victoria.

“I don't know but I will look it up when we get back. Wow, it's strong, isn't it?”

The boys had taken their shoes and socks off, and were now trailing their bare feet in the pool.

“Come on,” said Karen. “Let's join them.”

Soon all four were cooling off. They began to feel drowsy, and one by one they lay back with their heads on the soft grass, their feet still trailing in the water. Gradually they drifted off into a quiet slumber. A breeze picked up. Rustlings could have been seen by the watchful eye, but not by these four children who were soon held in a deep sleep.

***

Christian and Olivia had walked further round the beach, but after a while also decided to head inland, and were now having similar struggles through a different part of the forest.

“Why have you brought me this way, Christian? You know I can't stand creepers and things. Ouch!”

“Look, Olivia, we're nearly there.”

“Where, for heaven's sake? You're doing this on purpose. I *hate* it here!”

“Can't you see, Olivia? Look, through the trees, there's a lovely patch of light, and it's only a few steps away.”

“What do you mean, only a few steps? I've gone enough steps for one day, thank you, and you're going to have to get me out of here!” At which moment, she glimpsed up ahead what Christian was talking about: a patch of light in the trees, as well as the sound of running water. Oh, thank goodness! I can take my beastly shoes and socks off and have a paddle.

Emerging into the clearing, Christian and Olivia were entranced by a dozen or so hummingbirds hovering round a tree covered in white blossom, darting from place to place, sipping its nectar.

"Wow!" whispered Olivia, completely forgetting her discomfort and moans of a moment ago. "Isn't it beautiful? Oh, Christian, did you know this was going to be here?"

"Of course I did," he replied, not quite truthfully but eager to please and appear impressive. "I knew it wouldn't be far to go."

They were facing directly into the sunlight, so the pool ahead was a mirage of dazzling rippled yellow and green light. They had to shade their eyes it was so bright and then they also were overcome by the heady scent of blossom.

They sank to the ground by the pool and Olivia began scooping up handfuls of cool water which she splashed onto her face. "Oh, how wonderful!" she said between sloshes. "Come on, Christian, it's gorgeous!"

While they were sploshing and splashing themselves – and each other – they heard some giggling from somewhere nearby. At once they stopped and tried to peer ahead, but the light reflecting off the water was so bright they could hardly see a thing.

"Who's there?" called Christian, and a voice called back, "It's us."

"Who's us?"

"Karen, Vicky, Zak and me, Corey."

"How did you get here?"

"Same way you did, I expect, through the jungle." More giggles from across the water.

"Come on, Olivia, let's go and find them."

They walked round the pool, enjoying the verdant lushness of the vegetation and admiring the waterside ferns and grasses.

"There they are!" exclaimed Olivia, and she bounded over to the foursome who appeared to have been rolling over in the grass, were covered in leaves and crushed white blossom and were giggling uncontrollably.

"What's so funny?" she asked.

"We've been playing leap-frog," said Corey, "and Karen leapt over Zak and ended up in my arms, and Vicky leapt over Corey and fell into Zak's arms, and that's how it is, I guess."

Christian and Olivia looked amazed.

"How has this come about? Karen, what's been going on?"

"Well, I don't exactly know," said Karen, "but I must have been asleep and when I woke up, there was Corey, and, well, nobody else sort of mattered. I can't explain it, but somehow it is all okay now."

"Well," said Olivia, and at a total loss for words simply repeated, "Well" and then, realising how happy she was for them, "That's great. And we're okay now as well," she said, turning back towards Christian.

"What happened with you two?" asked Zak.

"It was just a bit of a misunderstanding but then we had a chat on the beach, and you know how you only need to talk and things can get sorted out. Well, that's how it was for us. And so we took a walk, and somehow ended up here: Lovers' Rest!"

"Lovers' Pool!"

"The Pool of Romance!"

"Come on, before we get too corny," said Christian. "It's time to go back and see how everyone else is getting on."

***

Together, Graham and Helen had been working on steps three to six of 'how to make panpipes'.

Step three

Sand the bottom end of each tube until it is rounded. Put the wax in the kettle and melt it. Place the sanded end of the bamboo in the melted wax. After the end is plugged, drizzle a little of the wax into the tube, and swirl it around on the inside to coat it and create a moisture seal on the inside of the tube.

Step four

Sand the mouth-piece end of the tube until the outer edge is smooth, but leave a sharp edge on the inside rim. Swirl some wax over this end as well.

Step five

Check the tone of each pipe by blowing across it as if you were blowing across a pop bottle opening. Fine tune it using an electronic tuner that will place an indicator light at the closest note. When you are satisfied with the tone of each tube, place the tubes in order on a holder such as a notched board to hold them in place while you fasten them together.

Step six

Thread a large needle with heavy twine. Weave it in and out around the pipes. Pull the twine until it holds the pipes firmly, but not so tightly that it will crack the bamboo. Seal the knot with a drop of wax or glue.

They didn't have a kettle for melting the wax, so they had to light a small fire and use a saucepan instead. They were extremely methodical every step of the way, and eventually had made one set of panpipes. Now the big test was to test each pipe for tuning. Graham had brought a tuning fork, fortunately, but would the pipes match the tuning of his 'cello? Helen had been very careful with her measurements the day before, so they hoped for the best.

“They're not quite perfect,” remarked Graham, whose sense of pitch and tuning was very acute, “but they're near enough. Anyway, you wouldn't want them to be pitch-perfect, I don't think, it wouldn't sound quite natural. But they make a beautiful sound, don't you think, Helen?”

“I am really pleased! Oh, I really wanted to make these, and now I have. I'm going to ask Maia to decorate them with nice swirly patterns. Come on, let's make another set.”

8
Music and Transformation

Captain's Log

So here is my report on Day Three of our Island Adventure, if I can call it that, because really it is turning out to be an adventurous – well, no 'adventurous' isn't really quite the word. (Hang on, I am going to ask Alice, she's clever with words – she won't be asleep yet...)

... Back now. She and Becky came up with 'transformative' which means making a change to one's life. Alice also said 'metamorphosis' was a good word, because that meant changing from one state into another, like a chrysalis changing into a butterfly. I didn't know that one, and anyway I thought that might be going a bit far. I like 'transformative' so I will stick with that.

The day started with the great storm which Tom had been practically praying for. I think he had been doing rain dances, and it was a pretty good one, but not quite strong enough, to completely wipe us out. David will have some great footage of it, and he has told me about his idea of making a proper film one day with Oliver's father's help, of course – he's full of ideas, is David. But I reckon his own filming will be enough, and anyway we will never be able to recapture this experience. Maybe Oliver's dad can help him edit what he's taken and turn it into a great movie: up for 'Best Foreign Film', I reckon!

Anyway, to get back to the day. We recovered from the storm, cleared up the mess, had a meal then went off in groups to do whatever we wanted. We re-assembled at four p.m., and had a swim, followed by volleyball, like yesterday, which was great, then another swim to cool off, and finally we had a brief chat together about the afternoon's activities, because I had to meet the member of staff who was coming with supplies at around six p.m. and tell them how we were getting on.

Alice told us about some strange incidents at the play rehearsal, such as falling off logs, and being stung by ants, and sinking into bogs – it was difficult to know whether these were just ordinary things, or extraordinary, if you see what I mean.

"Well, they seemed a bit odd at the time," said Alice, "because although I am a totally rational person, even I felt a funny sort of presence there, as though something or somebody was sort of playing around with us or, to put it better, playing *with* us. I know they sound like perfectly normal things such as might happen anywhere, but at the time they did feel a bit different, that's all I can say."

"What do you think, David?" I asked.

"I think I have to agree with Alice, because in a way I don't believe in spirits at all, but then I would like to as well, and it's a bit of a curious mixture this place, and I can't get my head round it, so the answer is, I don't know what to think."

"Anyone want to add anything?" I asked.

"All I know," said Lucy, "is that nobody got seriously hurt or anything, and we all survived the storm this morning, so I don't believe anything harmful is going to happen to us on this island. We are respecting it, and so it is respecting us, but it is having a bit of fun with us at the same time, as well as giving us a good time."

Everyone seemed happy with this, and Lucy always comes out with something pretty sensible, so we left it at that. I then asked Helen and Graham how they had been getting on.

"Look what we've made!" said Helen, and they produced from behind their backs two sets of panpipes, and immediately jumped up to play a duet. Wow! It was stunning, and had us all totally entranced. Soon we will all have a musical instrument to play. All we need is an island song, like an anthem, and this gave me the idea that we could write a class song like we used to do in English lessons.

So I immediately announced, "Look, everyone, let's write a class song, and get Zak to set it to music."

This was greeted with general approval, so we immediately made a start. (I was first Scribe, and the idea is that you pass being Scribe on to the next person after a few minutes, while everyone else comes up with lines, and gradually the poem, or song, gets written – you'll get the hang of it.)

"Zak, give us a refrain, and a beat, to get us going." Which he did by strumming on his guitar, preferring to do this rather than offering any lines or words which was not always his strong point.

Then the lines started coming out in a random kind of way but the rule is that you must let each person finish what he or she is saying, then someone else can improve on it, and then someone else offers a different idea, and then another chips in with a rhyme, and so on, quite noisily but creatively, and out of this 'brainstorming' as Pickles (our English teacher) liked to call it, a poem emerges. We'd done some great ones in the past, so it would be even better here, I reckoned.

Well, we had a pretty noisy lively session, and we all ended up on our feet, stamping out the rhythm in the sand, occasionally knocking each other around, pushing each other over sometimes, but it was great fun and this is what we ended up with:

From far distant lands
We've flown across the ocean:
To this island full of joy
We offer our devotion.
We've found a haven here
Of happiness sublime,
A life-transforming week
Enduring for all time.
Golden sands, pink sunrise,
Swaying palms, deep blue skies
We'll treasure evermore
Our days upon your shore.

Perhaps it wasn't our best ever, and Zak said it wasn't the kind of thing he would ever set to music ("too rhyme-y and corny for me") but by adding a few 'la la la's' here and there, and loosening it up a bit, he would do his best. Graham and Helen will add harmony with 'cello and flute, there will be panpipes to blow, and percussion as well, so I reckon it will be a great anthem.

End of day's log.

***

"Karen?"

"Hmm?"

"How are you feeling now?"

"Happy, relaxed... just great. And you?"

"About the same."

"You remember when we read *A Midsummer Night's Dream*?"

"I was just thinking about that. How weird! But it's like us, isn't it, sort of. Demetrius wanted Helena, Corey wanted you, Lysander wanted Hermia, Zak wanted me, and that's how it's worked out, but without all the misunderstandings and chasing around in the fog."

"Yes, there was all that muddle in the play, but here there wasn't. It was as though they got it right first time – whoever *they* are! Do you know what I mean?"

"The other funny thing is that Helena was taller than Hermia and you are taller than me."

"I know, it's just too weird for words. So what do you think's going on here? And what's going to happen next?"

"I have absolutely no idea. But never mind, 'what will be will be', as my mum says *all* the time. Sleep now, eh?"

"Okay, night night."

***

"Tom?"

"Yes."

"Will you come with me and David tomorrow to the top of the mountain? You can do your weather stuff up there, can't you?"

"Yes, of course I can."

"I really want you and David to witness what was going on, when I couldn't get to the top."

"Well, it was a bit like me when I was scrambling over those rocks, remember? Maybe wise guy David will have some ideas. There's certainly something a bit odd about this place."

"Are you enjoying it, though?"

"Of course I am! This is the coolest time I've ever had in my life – and the hottest! Oliver?"

"Hmm?"

"What's going to happen, I mean, after we get back, and it's the end of term?"

"Hmm. I dunno. I can't think about it. Something will work out, I expect."

"Hope so. Okay?"

"Okay."

***

"Graham, do you mean?" said Olivia.

"Yes. I know we've always dismissed him as a bit of a fool, and a joker, but you know, when he was helping me with the panpipes, I saw quite a different side of him: really concentrated and focused just like when he plays his 'cello. He was quite different, and... well, I don't know, but he was just so nice, and yet sensible. But still fun."

"Well, I'm glad you like him, Helen. Is he just shy, do you think?"

"Yes. I think all that jokiness is just a cover."

"Perhaps you'll be able to bring him out of his shell! It's funny what's going on here, isn't it?"

"Hmm – but it's great. I'm loving it, aren't you?"

"Course I am – heaven! Heaven on earth! Night night."

"Night night."

***

"I'll have it finished by tomorrow," said Philip.

"And what will you do with it then?"

"I will announce it to everyone, and we can go up the mountain with it. But we will have to find some good strong stakes first, to mount it on."

"Is it going to be a kind of mascot?" asked David.

"Yes, that sort of thing. It will be our answer to *Lord of the Flies.*"

"Brilliant! It will be hilarious! And we can dance around it, singing our island anthem."

"I hope Zak writes a good tune for us. Our class poem was pretty crummy, I thought. Well, not crummy exactly, but not quite right for a tropical island."

"Yes, I think we all felt that. It's so different here from school, and all we could come up with were boring rhyming couplets, or quatrains, or whatever they're called. But Zak's pretty cool. He'll transform it with a touch of his special magic, I reckon."

"Hope so. Good night."

"Good night."

***

"Of course I like her!"

"So what are you going to do about it?" asked Zak.

"Well, you know me, I just get tongue-tied and that's why I go all stupid and start loafing around, joking and giggling – you know what I'm like, Zak."

"Yeah, mate, you're hopeless, really. Ouch, that hurt!"

"Serves you right! You're going to have to help me, not just lie there making idiotic remarks."

"Okay, I'll come up with something. Helen and I are going to work on this song thing, or anthem, whatever it is, tomorrow. Don't worry, mate, I'll slip in a good word for you."

"Cheers, mate. G'night."

"G'night."

***

Maia and Lucy were lying on the sand under the stars, holding hands and quietly humming to the night sky. They had been for a surreptitious late evening dip, and were now calming down before bed. They had seen fireflies among the palm trees, and then the moonlight and the stars had been reflected in the small bubbles on the water's edge. It was all too romantic for words. Now they were singing an accompaniment to the wind's rustlings overhead. Later in their lives, they would return to this evening - the sheer bliss, and wonder, and peace of it.

9
Surprising Discoveries

"I haven't told you this yet, Corey, or anyone, come to that."

"What's that?"

"They want to visit us."

"Who?"

"Our parents."

"No, no, no! That was the deal, that we would be alone, absolutely by ourselves, for five days and five nights. They knew that, and they agreed to it."

"Yeah, I know, but... the thing is, on the final day when we're collected, they want to visit us in the morning, and just take a look for themselves. I can understand that. And by then it will practically be over anyway. I know we don't have to leave the island until the end of our last day, and then we're having one night in their hotel ('rehabilitation' they call it!), but still, I think it would be kind of hospitable. After all, they have paid for all this."

"Hmm. Well, you'll just have to see what the others say. I suppose we could put on a bit of a show for them – you know, sports and stuff."

"And then there's Alice's play."

"Yeah, that's true."

"And we could sing them our anthem."

"Hmm, okay, you're beginning to convince me. And at least they can take some pictures… okay, let's sleep on it."

"Good idea."

***

"Becky?"

"Yes?"

"I've been thinking about your writing."

"What have you been thinking?"

"Well, if you wrote the story of us being castaway on this island, you will need to know everything about everyone to make it a proper, full account."

"What do you mean?"

"Well, you don't know exactly all the stuff that's been going on, you know, between Zak and Karen, and Victoria and Corey, and then there's Lucy and Maia, and Tom and Oliver. I mean, we all know about it, but it's all a bit hush-hush in a way, but for the story to be complete and real, you should include all that, don't you think? And there's also Olivia and Christian."

"Gosh, you're an observant one, aren't you?"

"It's just that there's been a lot of change, even in only three days."

"And who knows, more may be in store, eh?" Becky said with a laugh. "You're right, Alice. I'll have to interview everyone, and get their different viewpoints, and stories, then put together the whole picture and write my first novel. How wonderful! I shan't be able to sleep now."

Day Four

Unusually, Christian called a meeting after breakfast to announce what he had told Corey last night. After an initial display of outrage from some and even bad temper from others, gradually he managed to calm them down. “I understand what you're all saying, but let's be a bit flexible and reasonable. Things are changing every day on this island, and I think we need to go with the flow. I only heard this from Mrs Thompson yesterday, and she was really quite pleasant about it. She realised it was breaking the agreement, and said that it was entirely our choice and our parents would go along with our decision. But she also pointed out that it would round off our week in a celebratory way.

“Alice has got a play to perform, and Corey has been working on a sports programme, and we've got some songs to sing and I know that Philip has got something up his sleeve as well which he wants to announce later today. I also think we could show them round, and talk about our projects. And they might agree to give us our mobiles so we can take some pictures at last.”

That was the clincher: to have their mobile phones back! A cheer went up, and cries of, “Yes, yes!” “Let them come!” and “Make sure they're fully charged!”

“Okay. I will tell the staff later that we are happy with this, and we'll put on a programme for them.

So now I reckon we carry on as before, and now we've got two days to put it all together."

It certainly gave a bit more edge to the morning, knowing that there was a deadline to meet and an audience to please. They didn't like to think that they were already more than half-way through their stay – this was too awful to contemplate – so they set off, no singles any more (apart from Philip who was always the independent one), and they would not report back for lunch until one o'clock to allow for a full morning's work.

***

No gourds had magically appeared overnight for turning into drums but Becky had another idea. She remembered the noise the pots and pans had made in yesterday's storm as they went careering across the beach, knocking into each other. There was her solution which she suggested to Graham.

"I can see what you're saying, but they don't look right. Supposing we cover them with creepers and stuff, to give them more of an island look. I don't know why we've got them anyway. We've never had to cook anything, the fire has really only been for fun."

"That's obviously why we've got them, then!"

So they spent the next hour disguising three large saucepans as tropical drums, and found a variety of sticks to hit them with, each creating a slightly different effect. Then they carried on with the coconuts: extracting the milk, cutting out the nut part and turning them into clip-clop instruments.

While this was going on, Becky very cautiously began her research, as she had discussed with Alice last night. By careful questioning, she gradually managed to highlight the main concern that was now occupying Graham's mind: Helen. Ah ha! The last thing she wanted to do was pry, but she didn't need to. Graham opened up to her in a way she would never have imagined. The island was weaving its spell over them all, and this would eventually provide her with a thread to follow through her book.

***

Tom, David and Oliver had battled their way through the dense jungle area beyond the beach and were now climbing up the mountain slope where Oliver had had his strange experience two days ago. It was mid-morning, the weather was calm, and there was no reason to imagine why they would not be able to reach the top in less than half an hour. Occasionally they looked back to enjoy the view of distant palm trees and coastline and turquoise sea beyond. It could hardly have been a more serene outlook.

"I think we shouldn't assume anything, either good or bad, about this place," said David. "It is only an island, after all, and is therefore basically inert. I don't want to disappoint anyone, but there are only spirits in the spirit world, and this is the earth: totally mundane and ordinary."

"But don't you think the world of the gods still mixes with the world of us mortals, as the Greeks did?" asked Tom. "They had priests, and we have church people, and they're supposed to stand between us and the spirit world, aren't they, interpreting things and looking for signs, and so on. What's the difference?"

"Even the priests in Greek times kept getting it all wrong just as our lot probably do. It's better simply to look at the facts, examine the evidence and come to your own conclusions. But I hope I'm proved wrong. I would love to see some hard and fast evidence of spirits roaming around on this island but it doesn't look very likely on a day like this, does it?"

"Why?" intervened Oliver who had been interested in the discussion so far. "It was just like this when I heard my flutterings, and had that funny sense of not getting anywhere."

"Well, we're getting somewhere now. We've practically made it."

Fifteen minutes later, after the climb had levelled out considerably, the boys were at the summit. It was stony and bereft of any vegetation and of course there wasn't even a little cairn of rocks to denote someone had been there before. But in a way that made it all the more exciting, because they were possibly the first people to have reached the top. They didn't shout for joy, instead they took it very calmly and simply enjoyed their small achievement with an inner glow of satisfaction.

Walking around, at last they could see the full extent of the island on all sides. Fortunately it appeared to be more or less circular in shape – perhaps a bit longer north to south than east to west – and Oliver was pleased about this. "At least I can see the overall shape of it now. Do you think we will have time to walk down the other side? I am thinking of my map."

"Not if we're going to be back on time," said David.

"Also, I am a bit worried about those clouds appearing over the horizon," said Tom. "I think it's just possible we may be in for another storm later, so we'd better not stray too far afield."

They were aware how storms can spring up in a moment in these tropical climates, so it seemed risky to venture into the unknown. Oliver contented himself with sketching freehand what he could see, estimating distances, and putting in any landmarks visible to the naked eye. He recalled some old-fashioned maps he had seen in books which were clearly short on accuracy but were colourful and artistic. He decided his was going to be like one of those.

Meanwhile David was giving some thought to Philip's surprise object which was going to be revealed later in the day. He had asked him to look for a way of supporting it, but there was no obvious way since the hilltop was like the bald dome of someone's head. He tested the ground with the heel of his shoe – hard and unyielding. Maybe it would give a bit if there was some rainfall this afternoon, as Tom predicted; then they might be able to dig three holes and make a tripod with wooden stakes. It was probably the only way. They would have to return prepared with the right tools if his idea was to work. David pondered where would be a good place, how to do it exactly and what they would need; he enjoyed working out problems.

The three boys enjoyed the quiet peacefulness of their mountain-top, admired the views of the horizon shimmering in the distance on all sides, and basked in the still warmth of the day. There was no sense of urgency or rush, unlike much of their lives at home, and they spent at least half an hour simply enjoying the peace of the morning as they pottered around.

Tom eventually put down his binoculars and said, “Come on, it's probably time we were setting off – those clouds are definitely heading our way.”

***

Alice had no luck with spiders, but she did find an unusually large and fast-moving centipede which had crept out from under the rock she was sitting on, and this engaged her attention for a while. She made several sketches of it, as well as some written notes about how it moved and behaved: totally fascinating, she thought. Then she decided to see how Corey was getting on. She found him on the beach, surrounded by different sized bits of trees, and sweating profusely.

“Hi, Alice. You've come just in time, because I am getting in a total muddle here.”

He explained to her his idea of making four sets of hurdles which would be lined up down the beach for races. Four sets meant twenty-four hurdles which was a lot to make out of these jumbled pieces, and with their limited resources for shaping and cutting.

"But I think it would be a great idea, don't you, watching everyone flying down the beach. We can roughly pace out a hundred metres, and that will be our track. We'll have four sets of heats, two for girls and two for boys, then the winners of each heat will take part in the final. It will be so exciting!"

Alice agreed so she helped him sort out the wood into twenty-four piles. They quickly realised they would need even more from the forest. After about an hour's gathering they reckoned there was enough so they set to work. The difficult part was making the hurdles so that the horizontal piece would fly off if it was hit by a foot or leg, while the rest of it stayed upright. This took some working out, and there was a slightly different solution for each hurdle because no two were quite alike. Hmm, it was a big job which kept them busy for the rest of the morning.

***

Lucy and Maia had been told about the pool in the clearing by Karen and Victoria, so decided to spend the morning there. They also had to struggle to fight their way through the tangle of creepers and vines, but once they arrived they were captivated by the beauty of the place. For a while they simply sat with their feet in the water, listening to the sounds of the jungle all around them: bird calls, rustlings in the undergrowth, occasional high-pitched screeches, stirrings in the leaves overhead.

There was a vast log from a fallen tree on the left side of the pool, half of it lying in the water, covered in bright green moss. Lucy's attention was caught by this because of something moving very slowly along its length. She couldn't be sure because it was perfectly camouflaged, and only the occasional movement gave away its presence. "Maia, look!" she whispered. "Can you see something moving along that log?"

She pointed to where she was looking, and as soon as Maia spotted the creature, she gasped in amazement. "It's an iguana! I'm sure it is!"

The creature was bright green from head to tail, and had a short spiny crest along its back. The girls couldn't see the full extent of its tail which was hanging down off the log into the undergrowth, but it was unmistakeably an iguana. Its black almond-shaped eye seemed to stare across the water at them. The girls were held in rapt attention.

"Come on," whispered Maia, "let's draw it. It might dart off any minute."

Fortunately the iguana seemed to be in no hurry to dart away, content to bask in the patch of sunlight which fell onto its tree trunk through the leaf-canopy. Lucy had secretly hoped for a sighting like this but hardly dared believe it would happen.

***

Olivia could not begin to identify all the different marine life she had seen that morning. What she had enjoyed most was the coral: some were branching, some seemed to form mounds, while others were more like plates. Some had horns, others had tentacles; but whatever their shape or size, they all attracted a huge variety of brightly coloured fish which swam in and out of these structures as if they were their home. It was like a society, she thought, or maybe a city. Well, at least it was an underwater habitation, and if she was a good story-writer, she could make up a story of an underwater world purely based on the lives of fishes, and their watery neighbourhood. Perhaps she ought to suggest the idea to Becky: an underwater tale about tropical fish.

She and Christian had walked to the sea's edge earlier, their differences resolved – such a relief for them both. Christian had left his surfboard behind because this time he had a different aim in view.

"I spotted some dolphins beyond the reef while I was waiting for waves a couple of days ago, so I've decided to go out and swim with them."

"Are you sure it's safe, Christian?"

"Why not? We've been assured there are no sharks in these waters and I'm a strong swimmer. It's just too good an opportunity to miss out on. I've heard so many inspiring accounts of people swimming with dolphins. When will I get a chance like this again?"

"Okay. Just take care, that's all."

***

Karen and Victoria had stumbled across a grove of papaya trees, laden with reddish green fruit.

"Can you eat them straight off the tree?" asked Karen.

"No, you have to let them ripen first," said Victoria. "My mum puts them in a brown paper bag with a tomato at home. She says that they get soft quickly like that."

"They're very high up. What if you gave me a piggy-back? I might just be able to reach those lowest ones."

So Victoria soon had Karen on her shoulders, and with a slight twist Karen was able to remove one plump papaya from its stem and hand it down.

"They're way bigger than the ones at home."

"I don't think I can reach any more," said Karen.

"That's fine. We don't want to be greedy. Anyway, it's really only to show everyone. We won't be allowed to take it home anyway."

"Come on, let's see what else we can find."

***

Philip had increased his tally of bird-sightings to six. He would have to look them up in a better bird book once he was home, but he had a clear idea and picture in his mind of what they were, and he had also made a few pencil notes:

1) possible robin, but bright scarlet
2) something like a goshawk, ash-grey
3) a dove-like bird, orange

4) a fantail, grey, bits of white, brown underside
5) collared lory (personal favourite)
6) variety of hummingbirds

Quite a good haul. Now he was in search of the right coloured leaves: purple, red, green and yellow. To complete his project shouldn't be too difficult.

***

Helen had completed three sets of panpipes, and she and Zak were testing them out in pairs to see how well they blended. She had been careful to cut each piece of bamboo to the same length, so they harmonised quite well, despite the different thicknesses of wood.

"They make such a great sound, Helen. Natural, kind of. It sounds like the wind is blowing through them – do you know what I mean?"

"Yes, I do. I'm really pleased. They'll be my souvenir of the trip. (Pause). What will you take back as a souvenir?"

"Hmm, good question. I think it will be the songs I've written, both the poems and the music, all inspired by our tropical island."

"Will you make a recording of them?"

"Sure. Perhaps they can be used as the sound track for David's film."

"Wow, what a brilliant idea!"

"Shall we do a bit more music?"

***

So the Castaways spent the morning exploring, relaxing, talking – totally absorbed in their various activities, forgetful of the outside world and all its pressures of time, work and commitments. The island seemed to be a safe, benign haven where they could be themselves, as well as discover something about themselves and each other which life had hitherto not afforded them. It was more than a holiday – perhaps it was closer to a retreat – refreshing and reviving, giving them time and space to explore and discover whatever they wanted to, for themselves and each other.

10
Phigys Solitarius

They were more than ready for lunch by one p.m., and fortunately they did not seem to tire of their simple daily diet. Different varieties of fruit had been turning up each day, as well as tasty breads and cheeses, while honey and yoghurt had been fine as a dessert. They drank coconut milk, or fruit drinks brought over from the mainland, and nobody suffered sudden cravings for chips or pizzas, which was just as well.

"Christian," called out Tom. "Look, we're going to be swamped any moment."

Everyone turned and looked towards the ocean. Tom was right: storm clouds were sweeping across the darkening sea, the wind was picking up and soon there would be a deluge.

"Dive for cover!" shouted Christian.

They quickly gathered up the remains of the lunch, making sure nothing was left outside to perish in the rain, then ran for their tents. It was a close thing: a few moments later the storm was directly overhead, sending down vast drops of rain onto their fragile habitation. Christian and Zak abandoned their own tents for the kitchen tent, in an effort to ensure that everything was kept secure this time. Corey and Graham would have to cope as best as they could by themselves. The scene of quiet sunny tranquillity was now awash with water, and who could say how long the downpour would last?

***

In David and Philip's tent, there was a flurry of activity.

"Look, I know there's no room in here but what's the alternative? I can hardly finish this outside, can I, so stop whining and help me, okay?"

David looked at the curious shape in front of him, and said, "So what do you want me to do? And what is it, anyway? It looks like nothing on earth."

"Don't worry, it will be fine. I know what I am doing. The framework is finished and that was the hard part. We've just got to add the leaves now."

"How do you propose to do that?"

"With this," said Philip, producing a coil of wire from his small tool kit.

"What else have you got in there?"

"Wire cutters, staple-gun, string, glue, scissors. I had it all planned out, you see. Now what you can do is fix the leaves to the frame, so..." Philip demonstrated. "I'll do the head, which needs to be as accurate as possible in terms of colour, if you do the tail, wings and body. It's easy: green on the back and red on the front. Now come on, we must get started or it won't be finished in time."

"In time for what?"

“When the storm stops, and Polly makes her first public appearance.”

“Got it!”

Elsewhere...

Zak, who had his guitar slung over his shoulder before the storm broke, was working with Christian on the island anthem. They played around with the words in order to give them more of a calypso rhythm, finding inspiration from the savage wind and rain which was lashing at the canvas. “It's coming, it's coming!” and they stamped their feet to help them free the spirit in the song.

Beneath the raging storm, Olivia was still underwater in her city of fish, imagining her story, 'Coral City' or something like that, finding a plot line, establishing characters, giving them names. “Now at last I might be able to write a decent story,” she thought, “all from my own imagination.”

Tom was watching through the tent flap, occasionally turning back to write short descriptive notes in his All-Weather notebook. He had a strong descriptive style, and one day would be turning meteorology into a literary art form.

In the midst of thunder and lightning, rain and wind, Karen was quietly humming to herself, admiring the flowers she had gathered, carefully and gently arranging their pastel-shaded petals into her press.

Graham, alone, using the two piled-up sleeping bags and clothes as a chair (who has ever practised in such awkward conditions?), completed his scales and arpeggios and now turned to his improvisation: Island Suite for unaccompanied 'cello. A unique title, he thought with a smile.

Corey needed some time alone to plan tomorrow's sports practice. He would ask Christian for the whole of tomorrow morning, so that the programme would go smoothly on the final day. He hoped the javelins would be working properly by then (he hadn't tried them since two days ago), and he wanted to include discus-throwing (if they could make one, somehow) as well as running, hurdling and... wait! He had a sudden idea which he would need to ask Tom about later.

Alice reckoned she would need three hours more rehearsal time. In her session this morning with Zak, he told her of his plan to have the whole of the next morning as a sports rehearsal. She couldn't argue with this, but she just prayed that it wouldn't rain again on the following afternoon as it had today, because that was going to be her only opportunity. There was Phillip's thing, whatever it was, occupying everybody's mind at the moment so she knew tomorrow would be her last chance.

Maia and Lucy were massaging each other's feet.

Oliver was working on his map, and occasionally tickling Tom's toes... but it wasn't having his toes tickled that made Tom jump up and shout out loud, "It's over, everyone! The storm is over! And now, look at the sunshine."

Gasps of wonder and amazement. The sun, emerging from behind deep purple clouds, was casting a broad path of golden light across the sea. It seemed to shiver and shimmer across the water, dazzling the world again after being so rudely obliterated for the last two hours. The castaways were drawn to its brilliance like moths to a flame.

But while they were held by its spell, they heard another sound behind them. "Come and meet Polly!" cried Philip. The children all turned around and were now captivated by another sight which gladdened them even more because it made them laugh. High on the top of the pole which Philip was carrying sat the glorious brightly coloured *Phigys solitarius* – solitary like its maker – the collared lory of the South Seas, its green feathers streaming down abundantly, its purple head with crooked yellow beak held high, and David, filming, squawking like a parrot for all he was worth. They had their mascot!

Captain's Log

Olivia sometimes complains that I don't express myself very well. You know, that I bottle up my feelings. Well, she can't complain any more, because I have just been talking to her for the last hour or so in a way that I've never talked to anyone before. It's all been pouring out of me, my happiness about us, about the day, and about my sadness that our island adventure will soon be at an end.

I think I noticed this in the others too, I mean about how they are beginning to show their feelings in a new way, like a kind of release. It does make me think of *Lord of the Flies* because there the primitive nature of the island released all the kids' feelings but in a very negative and destructive way. Here it has been much more positive and healthy. I'm not sure I'm putting this very well, and it's at times like this I wish I was better at English. Whenever I hear Becky or someone like Tom reading out their stories in class I think, “How do they do it? Where does it all come from?” Oh well, I can only do my best. I'm sure you get the gist of what I'm trying to say.

Anyway, to get back to the log, and I must try and get it all in the right order which means, for me, starting with the dolphins.

You know what it's like when you've been away from home for a long time and you arrive back and your dog comes bounding up to you, leaping all over the place, treating you like a long lost friend. It's always like that for me when I come back at the end of term and our golden retriever goes bananas with excitement and licks my face until I'm sopping. Well, it was a bit like that with the baby dolphins – except of course they didn't lick my face! But it was as if they came to find me and not me them, if you see what I mean. It was just a wonderful feeling of friendship and affection, and then enjoying each other's company, bobbing around each other in the ocean. Now I do know that there has been a lot of adverse publicity about swimming with dolphins, so I was careful not to stay too long or try to touch them. And of course I didn't have a boat which might upset them. So I felt okay about it and it was a really nice experience and I'm sure I didn't harm them or upset them in any way.

I realised I had been very rash because I had swum a long way out and was already feeling tired and then I had to swim back again. But those few minutes were really amazing and wonderful, and I wouldn't have missed them for the world. So I have just been telling Olivia all about it and I think she was really pleased for me. I had already told her some of it when she found me stretched out on the sand, exhausted and recovering my strength. But she had been so thrilled about her snorkelling and all the amazing fish she had seen and the sponges and the coral (sorry, too many 'ands' there), I just lay there smiling up at her as she poured out her experiences because she had just had the same sort of feelings that I did and she just wanted to convey some of her own enthusiasm and excitement, so I just lay there and listened.

Eventually we returned because we guessed it was lunchtime and anyway we were ravenous. Gradually the others came as well and everyone had a lot to talk about but I'll come to that later on when we have our usual evening get-together and I'll try and remember some of the experiences they spoke about. There was nothing ordinary about any of it, and I think this is what makes it so special here: its extraordinariness, if there is such a word.

Anyway, we had lunch and then there was another tropical storm which sort of broke up the party, and this was probably quite a good thing because it meant we all had to rest until it blew over. Although it was noisy and windy with really heavy raindrops, we all felt quite safe in our tents. I tried my hand at music with Zak which I had never done before because I'm totally unmusical, I don't play anything and I can hardly sing a note. But Zak said that was silly. Everyone was musical deep down, you just had to open your mouth and tap your feet and "just go with the flow, man" - you know what he's like. Well, that was another big release moment for me because I followed his example and it just kind of happened. We totally transformed our corny class poem into something really fun and lively, and in the end we decided it was good enough to teach the others later. I'm sure they'll love it now. Zak said that I was a natural musician which really pleased me and so that was another thing I spoke to Olivia about later: what instrument should I take up? Should I join a choir? Well, she wasn't so sure about that, but at least it gave me some ideas for when I get back home. Exciting, eh?

The storm finally died down and we went out to see the damage, which wasn't as bad as the previous day. There was a lot of mess on the beach which would just blow itself away, but the main thing was that none of our kitchen stuff was lost this time. It is just amazing here how quickly a storm can rise up and blow like fury for a couple of hours, and then equally quickly just die away again as if it had blown itself out. As we emerged from our tents, the sun appeared from behind a big black cloud and it sent a wonderful shaft of gold light across the water, so bright that we all had to shield our eyes from the glare. So we just stood there and stared for a bit. Some people did a few stretching exercises, the clever ones like Maia and

Karen did cartwheels, and fortunately David could always be relied to keep the camera rolling. What a film this is going to be!

Now, as the leader, it was always in my mind, "What's going to happen next?" and for once I was totally lost for ideas: it was too early for supper, and I didn't think anybody would want to swim yet. I was just about to suggest going to play volleyball but I needn't have worried because at that moment Philip appeared from his tent, shouting in our direction, "Look, everyone!" and so we all turned round to look. He was hoisting something which was sitting high up on the top of a pole, and it seemed to be made of leaves because it was fluttering, and it was glowing in all bright colours in the sunshine and then someone finally realised and called out, "It's a parrot!"

We all rushed to look, and, you know, you've got to hand it to Philip, he is so creative and clever and he's always top in Design and Technology and says he wants to be an architect like his dad one day. While we gathered round he lowered the pole so that we could all stroke its feathers and pat its head.

He then explained: "It's a Lory, just like Lewis Carroll wrote about in *Alice in Wonderland,* you know, in the bit where Alice cries and because she is so big it turns into a great lake which they all swim around in. Anyway, the Lory is a native of these islands and I have already seen a few here but I had planned to make this model whether I saw any or not. Now what I want to do, if you all agree, is to take it up to the top of the mountain and put it on the top of the pole, as our mascot."

"What, do you mean like in *Lord of the Flies*?" said Karen. "That was so creepy when they stuck the pig's head on a stick."

"And then it all got covered in flies," said Victoria. "It was disgusting!"

"No, it won't be anything like that. It will be fun and anyway it's not a Lord, it's a Lory."

"Polly the Lory!" shouted out Becky, and so our mascot was christened.

"What does a Lory sound like?" asked Alice. "Does it have a song? Or a mating call?"

Nobody knew the answer to that, so instead we all made screeching noises which were vaguely like parrots, I suppose, and anyway it was pretty hilarious so we all fell about laughing.

"Okay, guys, I'll give you five minutes to get ready with the right clothes and trainers and stuff. Some of you might not have been through the jungly bit, so you'll need a jacket because it stings like hell through there, and then we've got to scramble up the mountain. Corey and I will bring the spades. Zak can bring his guitar in case we want a sing-song, and remember we've got to find some strong stakes for the tripod but that should be easy as we go through the jungle. Anyway, keep a look out as we go. What else, Philip?"

So I needn't have worried about what to do next as it was all taken care of. We set off in a few minutes, and it felt good to be on an expedition together, because we hadn't really done that yet. We all helped each other through the forest, holding back creepers and vines so they didn't spring back in someone's face, then helping each other over boulders and streams, it was really fun, and everyone was in a good mood. Once we got through there, it was easy going gently uphill – there were no paths, of course, but we could see the top easily, and some went quicker than others, but it didn't matter because we would all get there in the end. Some of the girls liked to look at flowers and creepy-crawlies and all sorts of other stuff on the way, and why shouldn't they? Everybody was free to do their own thing, and there was no bloody timetable to follow (sorry, I shouldn't have said that probably, but everything is always such a rush back at home, and we are always told to be here, or there or somewhere else at some particular time and you know, we just get so sick of it. I tried to have as few 'times' like that as possible on this week and I hope I've got it about right).

It was a bit of a problem getting Polly on top of her pole, but Philip's ingenuity and everyone else's brawn combined to raise her aloft on her perch and she looked great! (Of course, we will be getting our phones soon to take some pictures – what a great idea of our parents to come and see us on the last day! It is really keeping us on our toes, as well, and we will put on such a day's programme as they will never forget for the rest of their lives!) She almost looked alive up there, and somebody even shouted out, “Don't fly away, Polly!” to which some wise guy shouted back in a parroty squawk, “Don't worry, I won't!”

"Right, guys," announced Zak when we had all stood around long enough. "Join hands, form a ring round Polly, and we will sing our Island Anthem. You remember that one from the first day? It went like this," and he strummed a bit, and sang a bit, and it all came back to us. In case you've forgotten, here it is again:

Boys (refrain):
Ba ba ba ba ba ba
Ba... ba... (continue while girls sing verse)

Girls: *Island of our dreams*
friend of our soul
you are one with us, you are one with us
in sleep and in waking
in memory, in forgetting
you are home for us, you are home for us.

Girls (refrain):
La la la la la la
La... la... (continue while boys sing)

Boys: *Radiant sunshine*
sparkling waves
vibrating with light, vibrating with light
a place of magic
and heavenly bliss
We've found our home, a home of delight!

Oh wow! (Not official logbook language, I know, but it was just so cool.) I took over the video cam so that there should be a few frames of David in the film, and he completely lets his hair down when he gets going, and he's so funny to watch, you would never think he was such a nerd. Anyway, the sight of us joining hands in a circle singing and dancing round a pole with a parrot on the top, on the top of a mountain on a tropical island (too many 'on's' there sorry!) was just so hilarious and so unique, and of all the highlights of the week so far, this must have been the biggest highlight. When we finished, we collapsed in a great heap of hysterical childish kids, which is what we were, I suppose: just a pile of kids having the time of their lives. So it could be done, I told myself, it could be done...

Philip came over to me and said, “My idea is that we will just leave Polly here as a perpetual reminder to the island – what I mean is, a memento that we came here once, had a great time and this is our little farewell gift. I know it won't last five minutes in a storm but let's just say that its spirit will live on. How does that sound to you?”

“That sounds just fine, Philip. Listen, everybody,” and I repeated what Philip just said and they were all pleased with his suggestion. In fact they burst into a round of applause and Philip took a bow which was quite funny to watch.

11
Prepare for the Finale

"Right, everyone," I said in my leader's voice (but I have to say I'm trying not to be too bossy-sounding but someone's got to take charge, haven't they?). "Time to go back now and have a dip in the ocean. I for one am sweating like a pig so let's go and wash it all off, eh?"

There was a general cheer and we all bounded off down the mountainside in our own time. Corey, Philip and I made sure the area looked tidy by smoothing out the ground where there were signs of digging holes and people's footprints, etc.

"That was great, Philip," I said to him. "You couldn't have sprung a better surprise on us, and it was a really cool class activity to come up here altogether and sing and dance around our class mascot."

"Yeah, great, man!" said Corey and gave Philip a great slap on the back which nearly sent him flying. "Oops, sorry, mate!" he said, catching hold of Philip just in time. "You okay? Don't know my own strength sometimes."

"Yeah, I'm okay. Is that everything then?"

So with the spades slung over our shoulders we made our way back down the hill whistling and singing as we went. The sun was getting quite low in the sky by now so we didn't hang around in case we missed our swim. We knew the way pretty well through the forest by now. The first thing we did when we got back to camp was to sling the spades down, quickly change into our swimsuits and head for the sea. By the time we arrived some of the kids had already had their dip and were drying themselves off.

“Tom and I will get supper organised now,” said Oliver, running up to me across the sand, “and we'll also light the fire because it will get cold fairly soon. But no rush, the water's fabulous so just go and have a nice leisurely swim and cool off.”

I wasn't able to be that leisurely because I had to keep my appointment with the members of staff and their daily check-up on us. Zak came with me, and it was the Thompsons this evening. We told them that everything was fine as usual (I get the sense they're fed up with us saying everything's fine, but what else can we say when it is?), and that we were happy for our parents to come on the last day and that we were preparing a programme for them to watch. But it was on condition that we would all be given our mobiles, fully charged, so that we could take some pictures. They agreed to that, of course, because they didn't have any option! How they were going to get here in that little ferry I had no idea, but that would be for them to sort out. We thanked them for a fresh supply of food and said goodbye at the jetty before rushing back to camp because we were half-starving.

Later on, when supper was over, I went round various people and chatted to them about the arrangements for the following day. So when everyone had cleared up, the washing-up been done and we were gathered round the fire, I just had a few words to say. "It seems as though we've all had a great day, and in case you don't know, Becky is going to write a book about it all. She's always wanted to write a novel and this is going to be it. So whatever you want her to include, you must tell her all the things that have happened to you and then she'll put them in her story. It will be more interesting like that than just keeping individual diaries. We all know what a great writer she is and she will make a fabulous book out of it. But as you know, we're seriously running out of time so I must leave it to each of you to chat to Becky in the next couple of days before we leave and she will make notes on everything you say, and make sure she includes it all. Is that okay with everyone?" And they all seemed to be happy with this because it would save them a lot of trouble of writing it all up themselves which can be rather boring.

"Right, now, as far as tomorrow is concerned, Corey wants to rehearse the sports programme in the morning, and he will want your full cooperation so that it runs smoothly and we can put on a good programme for the final day. Then in the afternoon, Alice and her cast will go and rehearse the play until it's ready and again she will want your co-operation but I know you'll all give her that. The rest of us can work on organising a programme for when our parents come the next day. This will include the sports, the play, going up to the top of the hill, singing our songs, playing any music that's been composed in a sort of concert I suppose, and showing off anything and everything else that we've done.

"I know that some of the things we wanted to do haven't happened but hey, who cares? The great thing is just to enjoy our final day of independence and island-living before we have to return to normal boring life. (I shouldn't say boring really, but it won't be quite the same, will it?)

"Now before we finish for tonight, Zak and I have rewritten our class poem, 'loosened it up a bit' as he likes to say, and so we would like to teach it to you."

This was met with general approval, and Helen, Graham and Becky handed out the various percussion instruments and panpipes which had been made, then Graham and Zak got their 'cello and guitar ready, because for this song there was going to be an instrumental introduction before the singing started. Everyone had something to hit or play or blow, Zak gave us the beat - and off we went.

Now I'm sorry I'm not clever enough to write down exactly what it sounded like, but all I know is that in the evening atmosphere, with the crickets chirping and the fireflies flickering in the trees, a gentle breeze blowing, the waves lapping on the distant shoreline and the moon coming up, it was the most atmospheric experience of my life. Here anyway are the words we sang, and at least David has got it all recorded with sound on his video cam – 'immortalised', to use his very own words. It doesn't look much on the page because it's meant to be sung not written, but this is roughly how it went:

Waway wawa way
we've flown away
far far far far away
we've flown across the ocean
and we bring our devotion
Wawa way wawa way
Chorus:
Blue skies
swaying trees
sunrise
balmy breeze
la la la la la la
Rororor we've come ashore
rororor for ever more
oh happiness sublime
beyond space and time
rororor for ever more
Chorus:
Blue skies
swaying trees
sunrise
balmy breeze
la la la la la la

So we now have two songs to sing. One of them will come at the beginning of the programme, and one at the end. (Gosh, it makes it feel like the Olympic Games with an Opening and a Closing Ceremony!) We will practise them both tomorrow.

By now I was totally shattered, and I think everyone else was as well.

I just had one more thing to say. "End of another great day, guys, you might give a moment's thought to anything you still want to do tomorrow, because we haven't had a discussion this evening, but I reckon it's too late for that now, and we're all pretty well dead-beat. But have you done enough to complete your projects when we get back home? That's all I mean. Anyway, good night and thanks for everything, island, or whoever you are!"

End of Log

"Are you happy about the play, Alice?"

"Yes. The main thing is that everyone knows their lines, and they know when to come on or off. Tomorrow we will go straight into a dress rehearsal, and any problems we can sort out as they occur. I am sure it will be fine. My only instruction will be that everyone needs to act as funnily as possible, because basically it is a weird comedy so the audience needs to laugh."

"Good idea."

"What about yours?"

"I have quite a few interviews to do in the morning, but I think there will be a lot of hanging around while Corey sorts out his Island Olympics so I will be seizing every opportunity to ask questions. I know everyone will help out with interesting answers; they've all got such big egos they will all want to feature as much as possible in my book!"

“What's it going to be called?”

“It could just be *The Castaways* – what do you think?”

***

“The only thing we haven't got are discuses. I can't figure out a way to make them, but it's a shame because they were one of the most important sports in the ancient Olympic Games. Have you got any ideas, Christian?"

"Well, I do have one idea, but you might think it's a bit stupid."

"What's that?"

"Boomerangs!"

"Hmm, I don't think that’s such a bad idea. Hasn't Tom been trying to make one?”

"Yes, I think he has, but I don't know if he's had any success.”

“I'll have a word with him in the morning.”

***

Maia was showing Lucy her paintings. “I have managed to do one complete watercolour each day which was my target. There are also a lot of sketches which I can work up into pictures later on if I want to.”

“You know what you can do with these, don't you?” said Lucy.

“What's that?”

“Becky can use them as illustrations for her book. They're so beautiful and they really capture the island in a way that no photograph will be able to. Even the sketches are lovely as they are. They have a sort of unfinished freshness and spontaneity – they really don't need any more work, to my mind."

"Really, do you think so?"

"I'll speak to Becky about it tomorrow if you're too shy."

"Let's go together, can we?"

"Sure, let's do that."

***

"I've just had an incredible idea," said Zak, suddenly sitting upright on his sleeping bag. "Hey, wake up and listen to this," and he gave Graham a heavy shove.

"Give over, I'm asleep."

"No, you're not – listen. You know all this music we've been composing. We've got two choruses now, you've written an unaccompanied 'cello suite (or at least part of it), Helen and I have written some music for panpipes and guitar, and I've got one or two other songs not quite finished. Well, my idea is that when we get back home we work the whole lot up into a CD, using all the funny percussion instruments we've made, and slip it into a plastic wallet in the back of Becky's book when it's published. You know how they do that nowadays. Don't you think that's a great idea!"

"I've got to hand it to you, Zak: it's brilliant. I mean, it's brilliant, man. But can we get some sleep now?"

"Sure thing, man."

***

"You know Becky's book?"

"Yeah."

"It's gonna need a cover design, yes?"

"Yup."

"What about your parrot?"

"Hmm. You don't think that would give the game away, I mean, because it comes as a surprise towards the end of the story."

"I don't think so. People will look at the book cover and ask themselves, 'What's that?' and I think it might entice them to read the book."

"Well, let's mention it to Becky in the morning and see what she says. My only concern is that it might well rain again before we get our phones back the day after tomorrow, because a tropical storm would ruin her in about two minutes."

"I think we're going to be all right now."

"What makes you say that?"

"Well, I just have a hunch that everything is going to play into our hands from now on. We've been trying hard to do all the right things, and I think that's gonna make a big difference. In my view, anyway."

***

"You know, Helen, I've always hated English because I've never been able to think what to write. He always puts on my report, 'Olivia lacks imagination and needs to read more widely.' Every term he says the same thing and it's so boring – but probably true. Anyway at last I've got a good idea for a story: tropical fish living in a city of sponges and coral. Isn't that wonderful!"

"Yes, it is wonderful but the only thing is, it's a bit late because when we get back to school we probably won't have to write any more stories."

"Well, I don't care, I'm going to write it anyway and make a children's book out of it. I bet it's never been done before and I will ask Becky for advice. She can proofread it for me or whatever you do. And I will do all my own illustrations. I've never been much good at art but Maia can show me how to do watercolours."

"I agree," said Helen. "I think it's a great idea."

"And what about you?" asked Olivia. "What's been best for you?"

"Working with Graham on panpipes and 'cello. I'd love to make a CD with him when I get back home. You think that's possible?"

"Why not? Anything's possible now, I think. What an amazing time we've had!"

"I wonder if anyone's ever composed duets for 'cello and panpipes. I bet they haven't. Don't you think that sounds really cool!"

***

"Look, Tom, there it is in rough outline, with a bit of guesswork here and there."

"Wow, Oliver, you've done that really well."

"When I get back, I'm going to turn it into a really beautiful map of our island, with lots of colourful details like the baby dolphins in the sea which Christian saw, and the waterfall..."

"... and the swamp which Alice got stuck in!"

"... and the lovers' pool in the clearing in the forest..."

"...and our camp, of course, on the beach..."

"...and the jetty where the staff came every day..."

"...and Polly on her perch at the top of the hill..."

"Yes, and I'll do small pictures like you get on the old-fashioned maps, and a picture of Neptune with his trident, and a North-South sign, and a few clouds in the sky, and palm trees, and there will be a fringe of sea round the edge with Christian on his surfboard..."

"...falling off!"

"Of course!"

"I hope this map of yours will go into Becky's book."

"Yes, it will. She's already asked me for it."

"Good. So you will be immortalised! Okay, Oliver, my hero! Are you ready for lights out now?"

"Yes, lights out now."

***

Victoria was lying back on her sleeping bag, with her head on her hands, when she heard Karen running back across the sand, opening the tent flaps and then falling down beside her. "Yes, she wants them."

"What, exactly?"

"She would like all our flower and butterfly pictures at the top of the page of each new chapter. She says that's what they often do in books: put illustrations on the page where a new chapter begins. So they will be quite small but will make all the difference, she said. She's also going to include some of her own pictures of dragonflies and newts, as well as Olivia's fish and Lucy's iguana pictures."

"Gosh, it's going to be as much of a picture book as a story book."

"And she said that our names would appear in the front of the book, along with Oliver's who is doing a map, and Maia's who she is hoping will allow her paintings to be reproduced. She's going to ask her about that tomorrow."

"Gosh, it will look quite wonderful when it's finished. And Becky will tell the story so well. I can't wait till it's in print. You really think it will happen?"

"Don't see why not. All our dreams have come true so far, haven't they?"

"They sure have!"

12
Mixed Feelings

Day Five

As it was nearly their last day, it had been suggested to Christian that they might sing the daily commandments for a change – could Zak set them to music? He discussed this with Olivia but they agreed it wasn't a good idea: they thought it was important to maintain their simplicity, and this might be lost if they sang them. So once again, after breakfast the following day, the castaways sat round in a circle and spoke together these words which everyone agreed had been such an important cornerstone to the week:

1 The Earth is our Mother. Care for her.
2. Honour all your relations.
3. Open your heart and soul to the Great Spirit.
4. All life is sacred. Treat all beings with respect.
5. Take from the earth what is needed and nothing more.
6. Do what needs to be done for the good of all.
7. Give constant thanks to the Great Spirit for each new day.

8. Speak the truth: but only of the good in others.
9. Follow the rhythms of Nature: rise and retire with the sun.
10. Enjoy life's journeys but leave no tracks.

Corey had been talking to Tom earlier about boomerangs: had he had any luck with them?

"Well, yes and no," and Tom ran off to his tent and came back with what he had made. He had used glue and string from Philip's toolkit to strap together two pieces of wood of roughly equal length, thickness and shape.

"So you see, it looks like a boomerang but it doesn't fly back to you. It just goes straight ahead and then falls to the ground. Look, I'll show you," and he threw it hard. It flew quite well but then suddenly plummeted to the ground.

"That's brilliant!" said Corey. "I haven't figured out how to make discuses so we will have boomerangs instead! Christian suggested it to me last night. It will be a new Olympic sport: boomerangs..."

"...which don't boomerang," added Tom.

"Well, that doesn't matter. It will still be a great event. Look, Tom, here's what you can do for me. There's going to be quite a bit of hanging around this morning while we set up the running track and the hurdles and so on. Could you go and collect enough wood with Oliver and then show them how to make their own boomerang? Then while they're waiting until I call them, they can try them out."

"Yes, that's fine," said Tom.

Corey was in his element for the rest of the morning. There was nothing he liked more than organising people and events and he knew that he could put on a really great programme. The Island Olympics: his dream come true! Over the space of the next three hours everyone had a turn at running round the track, hurdling, javelin-throwing (which now, for no obvious reason, seemed to be flying just beautifully – no surprise to David, however, who would have more to say about this and other things later), and boomerangs. Corey also included a boys against girls relay race. This suggestion actually came from the girls so of course it had to be included. Once they had found a suitable baton, the girls' team organised a practice for themselves: as there were eight of them, this meant going round the track four times, with each of them running half the track. In fact they had two practices because handing over the baton smoothly would probably make the whole difference between winning and losing. Then it was the boys' turn: although they appeared to be quicker, their handovers were not so secure, even after a second trial run.

"I think we will make the relay race the final event of the day," announced Corey when everyone had collapsed in a heap of exhaustion on the sand. "Anything could happen so it will be the grand climax to the programme."

"Can we go for a swim now?"

"Yes, come on, we're exhausted."

"Okay, okay, just give me a moment to see that I've got everything covered." (Pause while he looked at his notes.) "Yeah, that's everything, I guess."

A great cheer went up and everybody rushed back for their swimsuits and there was a general charge towards the sea. Even Christian left his surfboard behind so that he would be free to splash around and join in the fun. There won't be many more times like this in the near future, so let's make the most of it now, he thought.

The next couple of hours were spent in a very leisurely fashion: drying off in the sunshine (with plenty of sun-protection cream), something to eat, somewhere to sleep, the last day of no pressure, no adults, complete freedom to do what they wanted.

When she felt it was time, Alice rounded up her cast and they headed for their performance area where they would be taking the parents the next day: *Alice in Jungleland* was the play's new title, and this somehow liberated them to do what they liked with it, and allowed for any strange jungle peculiarities which might occur during the performance.

"What are we going to do about prizes?" asked Victoria. The remaining eight castaways were lounging on the sand when this question popped into her head.

"Hmm, that's a good point," said Christian. "Any ideas, anyone?"

"At the ancient Olympics they used to award laurel wreaths, didn't they?" mentioned Olivia.

"You're right!" said Corey. "They shouldn't be too difficult to make."

"How many will we need?"

"Well, let's see: there's the winner of the girls' javelin, the winner of the boys' javelin, the same for the hurdles, the same for the boomerang, and the same for the running. How many is that?"

"Eight so far."

"Okay. Then we'll need one more for the captain of the winning relay team, which makes nine. Who are the captains, by the way?"

"We haven't chosen them yet," said Christian.

"How about you being captain of the boys and Olivia being captain of the girls? How do the rest of you feel about that?" asked Corey.

"Seems cool to me," said Zak. "A bit of rivalry between the lovebirds – what do you think?"

The rest thought this was quite a funny idea, so Christian and Olivia nodded their assent.

"We'll get the better of you tomorrow just you wait!" she said to him, holding up a clenched fist to his face.

"Okay, okay," he said, flinching away. "We might have dropped our baton a couple of times today, but tomorrow we'll be like a smooth-oiled machine. You won't stand a chance!"

"Okay, let's keep the sparring till tomorrow, eh?" said Corey. "Who wants to make some victory wreaths?"

Graham, Zak and Helen all declined because they had some music to practise.

"That's fine. Suppose the rest of us look for some vines and creepers, that sort of thing, and bring back here what we find, then we can kind of pool our resources and try and make them while these guys entertain us with their music."

This idea met with general approval, so Christian went off with Olivia in one direction while Victoria, Karen and Corey went off in another, leaving the musicians to work on a new trio they had in mind.

Zak had written a poem which he thought had the makings of a folksong with guitar, 'cello and panpipe accompaniment. "The poem goes like this:

White clouds under blue skies
white waves over blue seas
rolling along, rolling along
Bright birds in the green trees
deep pools under forest leaves
creating my song, creating my song
Memories and dreams
sighing in the breeze
staying with us long – and ever more.

That's it, really – what do you think?"

"That's wonderful, Zak. It captures the atmosphere of the place," said Helen. "Don't you think so, Graham?"

"Yup, I love it."

"Good! Well, here's the tune and I'll just strum along and sing, and you join in whenever you like, and we'll see if we can make a trio out of it for when the others get back."

Within about half an hour, the others had returned with armfuls of creepers, and spent the rest of the afternoon quietly untangling them and turning them into victory wreaths while the musicians gradually got the tuning and rhythm right for their new song.

"So what will be the order of things tomorrow?" Christian asked Corey after a while.

"Okay, so this is what I've got in mind. I'm hoping that all our parents will be here by say ten o'clock, and we'll have them sitting in the shade of those trees on the edge of the beach. For the opening ceremony I am hoping that there will be enough of a breeze for Oliver to fly his kite while we sing the first of our island anthems. I like the idea of watching it flying around in the air while we're all singing. Then we'll have the first of the track events which will be the girls' running heats followed by the boys' heats; after that, the heats of the hurdles, then the javelin and boomerang finals (without heats, I think); and to finish, the finals of the track events, followed by the relay. How does that sound?"

"Are all the sports events going to take place in the morning?"

"Yes, I think so. I hope we'll get through them all by about midday or soon after, when we'll have lunch. Christian, when you see the staff later this afternoon you must tell them that our parents will need to bring extra food supplies because we won't have enough to give them lunch. Also tell them to bring a cushion to sit on if they want to and umbrellas as sunshades, and the right sort of clothes and shoes to wear through the jungle and up the hill later."

"Yup, I'll do that. Anyway, go on with the rest of the programme now."

"It's all fairly straightforward after that. Prizegiving is the next thing, so we must remember to appoint two parents to give out the laurel wreaths. My idea was to ask Christian's mum to crown the boys, and Olivia's dad to crown the girls. Is that all right?"

Everyone seemed happy with that, so Corey carried on: "When it's over, we sing the second island anthem and have the kite flying overhead again, and that will be our closing ceremony. Then it will be lunchtime, and we will all, I mean the eight of us here plus the adults, do the clearing up as well as all the packing away of tents and everything like that while the cast go and get ready to perform their play. Now my idea is that we can watch the play with our parents and afterwards we go from there up the hill to show them Phil's parrot. If we want, we can get in a big ring around it and by then our parents might be relaxed enough to join in the songs, and we can have a bit of a singsong and dance around the parrot."

"I can't see my parents ever doing that," said Olivia, "but I think it's a great idea."

"So do I," said Karen. "The whole thing sounds brilliant, Corey. I'm really looking forward to it now."

"Well," he said," I don't expect it all to go quite as smoothly as that. For all we know, there will be a tropical storm and the whole thing will be washed out."

"Don't say that!" said Victoria. "That's what they call tempting fate, isn't it?"

"Yeah, man," said Zak, "we've got to have positive vibes about this. Think positive and all that stuff, and then it'll just go great. The gods are on our side, and never forget it eh, man?"

"Sure thing," and there was a general round of high-fives.

Some of the laurel wreaths looked a bit peculiar with long dangling bits hanging down, but at least they all held together and in the end there were about a dozen of them which seemed enough.

"Look, is that them coming back?" said Helen. "Yes, it is."

Soon Alice and the cast of *Alice in Jungleland* had joined them.

"How did it go?" asked Christian.

"It's going to be fine," said Alice. "We went through it twice, and we've managed to cut it down to forty minutes which is quite long enough, because it's really hot and sticky in there. Anyway, we managed to 'loosen it up' a bit, as Zak says, and added a few jungle features and jungle creatures which makes it more authentic for the setting. For example, we don't have a Cheshire cat any more, we have a Cheshire tiger. And the March hare is now a March iguana, the caterpillar has turned into the giant centipede which I saw the other day, and the Mad Hatter is now the Mad Parrot! In fact, the whole thing is totally crazy."

"Brilliant" and "amazing" and "can't wait sounds hilarious" were some of the comments from the non-cast members.

"David is brilliant as the Duchess," said Becky. "He really should be an actor one day."

"But I am an actor!" replied David. "My whole life is one big act, haven't you ever noticed that?"

"And Lucy as the footman is now the most beautiful tropical fish you've ever seen, complete with fins and gills," went on Becky.

"By the way," said David, coming down to earth for a moment, "someone is going to have to do the filming. I can't for obvious reasons."

"Can I do it?" asked Graham. "I've never done anything like that before. I'd love to get in some good angles and close-up shots."

"Okay, everyone?"

Nobody objected, so that was decided.

"I've got to go and meet the members of staff now," said Christian. "Who's going to come with me? Corey, it'd better be you because you've got tomorrow's programme in your head. Who else?"

Victoria and Karen put their hands up.

"Great, thanks! So for the rest of you it's swimming, then supper and campfire, and singing and all for the last time, I'm afraid to say. So no hurry about anything, eh? Just relax and enjoy yourselves. We'll catch up with you later."

Captain's Log

Day Five: I was told I only needed to write up five days because the last day would just be packing, clearing up and going home. At the time we didn't know that we would be putting on a programme on day six, but I will leave that to Becky and her book, because she will make a much better job of it than I will.

So all we've done today really is preparing for tomorrow: the sports practice went okay, and Corey did his best to make sure it wasn't too boring. Anyway, we had boomerangs to make which was fun, and we all did some practice at the various sports. I think it's going to be a fabulous programme, and it will make the whole difference having our parents as spectators.

Then in the afternoon, while we made laurel wreaths, Alice and her crew rehearsed the play and we can't wait to see that either. Those will be the two main events, and after that we'll go up the hill, see how Polly's getting on, pay her our final respects, then pack up and leave. Sob!

After our final swim and meal, and we were gathered round the fire, Helen, Zak and Graham performed their trio which they had been rehearsing in the afternoon. And I have to say, it was really emotional: the tune was lovely, but sad and 'wistful' (that was Lucy's word) and they sang it slowly and after a couple of times we knew it pretty well. It went like this:

White clouds under blue skies
white waves over blue seas
rolling along, rolling along
la la la la
Bright birds in the green trees
deep pools under forest leaves
creating my song, creating my song
ba ba ba ba
Memories and dreams
sighing in the breeze
staying with us long – and ever more.
ma ma ma ma

Some of us, and not only the girls, were crying after that, and I guess I really felt it too. Nobody could say much then, as we watched the dying embers of the fire. There was quite a lot of hugging, and a bit of whispered conversation. The stars were out, the waves were lapping on the shore, the crickets were cricketing, or whatever they do, and the breeze rustled the leaves of the palm trees. Someone then pointed out our old friends the fireflies, so we watched them for a while among the trees. What a night to remember!

End of Captain's Log

13
Becky's Novel

If you haven't guessed already, this *is* my book – no great secret really. Christian allowed me to incorporate his logbook entries into it, but otherwise it's the project which I always wanted to do. It has taken me longer than anyone else's to complete, but I have finally done it. Except that it isn't a novel at all, because that would mean it isn't true, which of course it is. And for anyone who says, “It could never have happened like that,” or “It's all pure fantasy,” all I can say is it did happen and we are the living proof of it. I have called it a fantasy/adventure because it seemed at times too extraordinary to be true, and yet it is a true account of our form's leavers' week, and it will probably go down in the annals of Hengistbury Hall as one of the most memorable, I should guess.

So now I will tell you the rest of the story and whatever Christian says, it won't be any better coming from me, because he wrote his logbooks very well, in my opinion. The only advantage now is that I am not keeping a secret any longer, so I can really be myself.

There had been a storm in the night which amazingly some people claimed later to have slept through! But it was more rain than wind fortunately, so everything was more or less as we had left it the night before. Corey and others spent some time repairing the hurdles, but there was no serious damage. Soon everyone was free to have an early morning dip, followed by breakfast and our usual 'assembly', but for the final time. Gosh, that was an emotional moment, speaking the commandments, and I wasn't the only one who found it difficult to get the words out. The atmosphere of our circle was unusually hushed. In fact we had never spoken those words (which of course we knew by heart) so quietly, or perhaps with so much feeling. I saw a few people holding hands tightly for fear of breaking down, but we couldn't afford to cry because that would set everyone off.

"Okay, guys," said Christian, "I know what you're all feeling because I am too: dead sad, right? Well, let's just go along with it and know that's how we're feeling, but what are those French words, someone? You know, when you have to be brave when you've cut yourself and..."

David called out in a loud funny sort of voice, which made us all smile, "Courage, mon brave!" A few people laughed as well, and of course that helped.

"Yeah, that's it. So let's wipe away the tears and face the day, because it's going to be great and there's plenty to do. Lucy has had an idea, which I think's a really good one, so over to you, Lucy."

Dear motherly Lucy! I haven't written enough about her because there have been lots of little incidents where she has come to the rescue, not just with the odd cuts and grazes, but with tricky emotional moments where she has been there as the shoulder to cry on. You know how it is with some people: they simply are comfort and healing personified, if I can put it like that; a bit like our mums, I suppose, but Lucy has it in spades (I think that's the expression – it means 'lots of it'). Her gentle voice of calmness and sweetness came to our rescue at that moment as she stood up and spoke to us like a mother hen. “Well, everyone, this is my idea. We have got an hour or so before they arrive, so let's go and find masses of flowers and blossoms and make garlands out of them to put round their necks when they arrive. Philip tells me he's got lots of string left, and there are all those vines in the jungle which we can use. Then we can all go down to the landing place, which most of us haven't even seen yet, and be there when they arrive, and hang garlands round their necks.”

Brilliant! This was the general reaction and it would keep us busy while we were waiting, which is what we needed.

“Okay, everyone?” said Christian. “So go off in pairs or small groups, and come back here when you’re ready, and we'll pool our resources. Try and be back in half an hour or so.”

So that's what we did, and it worked a treat. There was masses of hibiscus and morning glory and frangipani, and we knew where to look for it by now, as well as some others which nobody could name. By the time we got back there were armfuls of wonderful blossoms, as well as some bits of creeper, and the ever-resourceful Philip gave us a demonstration of how to make a garland, using a simple method which he had just invented!

Only Zak was a bit reluctant to give it a try. “That's not my scene, man. Look, guys, can I play and sing to you instead?”

We all agreed that was a good idea, because it would be like music while we worked.

“Now we're going to have work quickly,” said Christian, “because there are thirty adults coming, including the Crawfords and the Thompsons, so that means about two garlands each. In fact, it's exactly two each, isn't it – well, anyway, we haven't got all day so let's get started.”

So while we worked, Zak sang his songs, and we joined in with the ones we knew, while others we just listened to as he made them up as he went along – improvised, I mean. He's clever like that.

After a while, Lucy had another word with Christian, and he interrupted the proceedings. “Look, Lucy says we can use whatever is left over to strew them around the spectator area over there.”

So by the time we finished we had enough garlands to go round, and a colourful 'grandstand' on the edge of the beach, shaded by the palm trees. At least it would remain in shade for the morning during the sports, and then we all set off for the landing.

I have already said earlier that not all our parents were able to come on this trip, and certainly some of our dads couldn't take time off work. So in all there were ten sets of parents, half a dozen mums and four teaching staff. My parents couldn't come for various reasons (which makes me all the more glad I wrote this book, for their sake), but I wasn't the only one so it didn't matter too much. Anyway, their hotel had arranged for a ferry to bring them, and we only had about twenty minutes to wait at the landing area before the boat came into view. We waved and waved when we saw them coming, and Zak had his guitar, so we sang for all we were worth. And the funniest thing was watching the adults walk down the gangplank thing to get off the boat onto the sand, helped by the crewmen of course, but still they all wobbled a bit, and it made us all laugh.

I don't know all the parents very well, but I knew the Adcocks, and the Nolans, and the Lannoys, and the Bradleys, and the Kenworthys, and the Seymours, and the Walkers. Then I recognised Mrs Mansell, and Mrs Bowden, and Mrs Rokison - and that was as far as my knowledge of names went, but of course I knew the others by sight even if I couldn't be sure who exactly went with who.

Anyway, it was a lovely arrival, and they all gasped with amazement at the garlands. It was so funny watching them put them on! David's got it all on film so we can laugh at it all again later. There were lots of hugs and kisses and plenty of embarrassment as well, and of course endless chatter.

We had agreed with Christian's suggestion that we shouldn't be given our mobile phones after all. This was a terrible disappointment to start with but as he had explained, "Look, we've been without them all week, so why don't we just let our parents and the teachers take photos, because you know what it's like: as soon as we are given them, we will be using them all the time, and it will totally distract us from the programme."

When he put it like that, we had to agree with him. Once we were on the mainland, and there was internet, we could use them as much as we liked, of course. But we had become used to not having them, although it seemed very odd for the first day or two. It was like a withdrawal, and some of the worst addicts found it really hard. But now it didn't seem such a big deal, in fact, it was a relief in a way.

For the next part I am going to become a sports commentator, because in a short while the day was turned over to Corey (who took centre stage) and the Island Olympics. (I will add at this point that the two-man crew of the ferry were invited to join in the day's proceedings as well, but heaven knows what they made of it all, particularly *Alice in Jungleland* – "totally mad, these English," they must have relayed to the families back home, I suspect.)

"Ladies and Gentlemen, welcome to our island, and our Olympic Games. We will begin with the Opening Ceremony."

Fortunately there was a light breeze this morning, so when Oliver made his dramatic entrance from under the palm trees on the side of the beach and threw his kite up into the air, the wind immediately caught it and sent it spiralling around in great arcs and loop-the-loops, carefully controlled by his guiding hands. We sang our opening chorus to the audience, and with the kite flying above the waves as our backdrop, it was quite an impressive start.

The girls' hurdles heat followed, and I took part in this. I can only say that I was hopeless, as I knew I would be, but I loved joining in and at least I didn't knock any of them over. The finalists were Helen, Karen, Lucy and Olivia. Then we sat down to watch the boys, and it was dazzling watching them racing down the track, leaping at full tilt over the hurdles and lunging for the finishing line. We all cheered but couldn't see who had won as both of the heats were really tight finishes. Mr Adcock who was on the finishing line announced the result. “The finalists will be Christian, Corey, Zak and Tom.”

Next came the girls' javelin, which would not be in heats but just a straight final. Victoria won this, probably because she had put in the most practice, and she had the strongest arms. I was equal last with Alice, which we thought was hilarious!

The boys' javelin was very exciting because it came to a very close contest between Corey and, surprisingly, Philip who you could see also had strong beefy arms. Watching them run up to the start, and then hurling themselves into their throw but not falling over the line, was really thrilling. The javelins wobbled a bit in the air, but at least they flew, and in the end it was Philip who won, beating Corey by inches on his final throw. They shook hands amidst great cheers from everyone.

Next came the running, which was the nearest we got to long distance: twice round the track was quite far enough in this heat. I had a bit more chance in this because I had staying power even if I couldn't sprint. At least I managed second place in my heat, so I got into the final. The other finalists were Maia, Victoria and Karen. (Poor Alice was no athlete, but at least she tried her hardest.) The boys' finalists were Christian, Corey, Zak and Oliver.

Now the boomerang came next, and this required a short explanation from Corey. “Ladies and Gentlemen, we were not able to make discuses but instead we have invented a new Olympic Sport with these boomerangs. Tom made the prototype, but unfortunately it didn't return to him as it's supposed to do. So we assumed it was going to simply be a distance-throwing event. However, since then, others have made better boomerangs which do return to them, or at least partially. So for this sport we have decided it will be for all-comers, which means you as well if you want, mums and dads, boys and girls, all against all. You will be allowed two throws, which includes one practice, and the winner will be the one who can make it come closest back to where they are standing.”

It was really funny watching everyone do this, especially some of the mums who really had no idea what they were doing and were wearing quite the wrong kind of shoes so had to take them off to make their run-up in the sand. But it didn't matter how far you threw it, just so long as it flew back to you. Most of the throws were hopeless, I have to admit, but sometimes the boomerang flew back at least some of the way and then it was great to watch. I don't know if there was any particular skill, more just luck, I think, but would you believe that the eventual winner was Alice! On her second throw, she simply closed her eyes, threw it for all she was worth, and the boomerang described a beautiful circle and practically clonked Mrs Bradley on its return. A great cheer went up, and Alice literally jumped for joy – her greatest sporting triumph – in fact probably her only sporting triumph ever!

Now we came to the finals: Karen won the girls' hurdles quite easily, because she had the best hurdle-jumping technique and the longest legs, and was a terrific sprinter as well. The boys' final should have been won by Corey: he was ahead but he stumbled a bit at the last hurdle, and Christian overtook him on the final stretch and claimed the prize in what was called a photo-finish.

I was up against Maia, Victoria and Karen in the running event. This was won by Maia, who had been saving herself, by keeping cool under the palm trees. She has a graceful style of running, never puffed or panted like the rest of us but seemed to remain composed and totally in control – very impressive. This is what the others told me later, because I couldn't really tell. In fact I got totally puffed out in the race and came last!

Christian, Zak, Corey and Tom made an interesting line-up for the boys' running: Corey was determined to make up for his hurdles blunder, Tom wanted to win one event if he could, Christian would want to prove that his hurdles win wasn't a total fluke and Zak probably couldn't care less, but "Hey! let's give it my best shot, man!" was probably his attitude.

He has real stamina, and although he was at the back of the field on the first circuit, as soon as the others started to gasp for breath second time round, he came into his own, picked them off one by one, just in time to pip Corey about ten metres short of the finishing line, much to Corey's surprise.

"Where did you spring from?" Corey asked, when they had collapsed in a heap on the sand.

Zak replied, "Outer Space – where d'you think?"

There was quite a long interval now, mainly for drinks, before the final event: the relay. There was no point in rushing into it, when most of us were so deadbeat. The adults needed to stretch and go to the loo, and have a general look round as well. We were still in plenty of time, and the sun hadn't come round either which would soon make it all too scorching.

After a bit, Corey thought it was time so he called out, "Okay, let's get organised for the relay, everyone. Just to tell you, we're all going to run half the track, so that means it will be four times round in all. Please can we have the line judges in position, and the starter?" It took a few minutes to organise, but then we were all ready.

Mr Nolan called out, "Ready, Steady, Go!" and we were off.

It all went by in such a blur of shouting and general excitement that it is difficult to recall everybody's run and all the detail. All I remember is that Maia ran like the wind on the first leg and gave us a good lead, then Tom put in a terrific sprint to catch up, then Olivia and Christian ran neck and neck which was quite funny. Then Zak absolutely flew on his turn, Karen caught up for the girls, Oliver fumbled the handover to Philip, giving me a chance to get ahead, handing over to Victoria for the last leg. She ran for all she was worth, but Corey was catching her up every inch of the way. In the end he just pipped her at the post, giving him his moment of glory. It was amazing! Sorry I can't think of a different word, but it was!

Then it was time for the prizegiving, but before that Christian's dad gave a great speech (which went something like this) once we were relaxed after all that excitement and the atmosphere had calmed down. "Thank you, competitors, for a fantastic Olympic Games. We never expected to be entertained like this, and you have put on a wonderful show. We, I mean your parents and your teachers, have been chatting among ourselves and two things in particular have struck us: first, that you all seem to be glowing with health and vitality (someone even said you look like young gods and goddesses!), and secondly that you all look so relaxed and happy. So, well done for making such a success of the week, and now we will crown the winners with their laurel wreaths."

So the prize-giving took place, followed by the closing ceremony: the kite flew above us while we sang the second island anthem. Graham played his 'cello, Zak on guitar, Lucy, Maia and Olivia played panpipes, and Helen played her flute; the rest of us did percussion with coconut shells and our funny drums made out of saucepans, so it was practically an orchestra. It made a curious mixture of sounds, but I think the adults loved it because it had all been created in the course of only five days.

"A wonderful show!" said Mrs Seymour. "Thank you very much. So now it is our turn to do something for you: we will prepare lunch, and we have brought some special food for you so go and have a nice long swim in the sea. Your last, I'm afraid, so make the most of it."

And we did! I have never felt so hot and sweaty, and I expect that goes for everyone. Christian wanted to show off to his parents his surfing prowess, but the rest of us were happy to swim and splash around in the waves.

The treat for lunch was chicken drumsticks and crisps, and slices of luscious if cold pizza and some veggie sausages for the vegetarians, so it was all very delicious and welcome. It would have been tempting to fall asleep under a palm tree for the rest of the afternoon, but there were things still to do.

"I suggest the cast go and prepare for their play now," announced Christian. "Meanwhile, the rest of us will clear the site and pack everything up, as much as we can, ready for leaving the island later on."

So we actors were happy to set off at this point and leave everyone else to do the clearing up – lucky us, to be missing that!

First of all, I will try to set the scene: we are acting on a fairly level piece of grass with a backdrop of trees. We had thought originally of having the audience on the opposite side of the stream which flows down from the small waterfall, but we realised that this would cause sound projection problems. So in the end we found a slightly tufty and rocky area on our side of the water which will serve as seating. We had warned the adults to bring cushions so that they would not be too uncomfortable sitting down for forty minutes. Of course there was no curtain or anything like that, but we had the deep darkness of the forest where we could change into our costumes as well as make our exits and entrances.

We spent a long time getting into our costumes and organising the very few props that we had, making sure, as far as we could, that nothing was going to go wrong as had previously. Everything seemed to be stable, there were no large ants that we could see, and we would be careful to avoid the one particularly boggy patch of ground that Alice got stuck in. Once we were ready, we hid among the trees and waited for their arrival. It wasn't long before we heard some conversation coming our way, so Alice went out to welcome everybody and point out where they should sit to watch. Soon everyone was quiet, and the play was underway.

Alice, who first of all had to climb up in the tree, began. "How boring it is sitting here with nothing to do. My sister (who is invisible by the way) is reading a book which has no pictures or conversations. What is the point of that?"

Enter Oliver along a nearby branch dressed as a white lizard (instead of a white rabbit).

"Oh dear! Oh dear! I shall be too late!" taking a watch out of his waistcoat pocket then hurrying on, then climbing down the tree.

Alice started climbing down after him but very slowly, saying as she went, "I wonder what on earth is going to happen next. And look at all the shelves and cupboards and maps and pictures – and look, what is this? A jar of orange marmalade – what on earth is that doing here? Hmm, empty, worse luck! I wonder how many miles down I've climbed by now? Am I near the centre of the earth, I wonder? Perhaps I will fall right through the earth and end up in New Zealand or Australia."

By now she had reached the ground.

"Where on earth am I? And what is this little bottle (which she found in the grass)? I think I'll take a drink and see what happens?" (She drinks from the bottle.) Oh dear, I seem to be growing taller and taller (she says as she climbs onto the stump). What on earth is going on? My feet seem to be disappearing from under me. Goodbye, feet! Oh dear, I think I'm going to start crying. (Alice starts crying.) Now control yourself, a big girl like you crying in this way, you should be ashamed of yourself. But I can't help it (and she carried on crying). And now look what you're doing: your tears are turning into a vast pool of water. Oh, and look, there's the white lizard again."

Enter Tom: "Oh! The Duchess, the Duchess! Oh! She will become so savage if I keep her waiting!" (Exit Tom.)

Alice: "Oh dear, oh dear. How queer everything is today. And look at all this water everywhere, oh dear, oh dear..."

In a moment, other members of the cast including me appeared on the scene, pretending to be jungle animals, and swimming around in the imaginary pool created by Alice's tears. The water level suddenly fell and we all stood on the imaginary river bank, shaking our fur and feathers, trying to get dry. A mouse announced that he would make them dry enough if they all would only sit still while he gave them a history lesson on William the Conqueror. This did not do the trick, so the Lory parrot (Philip, of course) suggested that more energetic methods were required, and the dodo recommended a Caucus-race. There was a lot of disorganised running around, then everyone sat down again, waiting for Alice to give out the prizes. And so on, and so forth, with scenes from the story which everyone knows so well: the advice from the Giant Centipede with the poem *You are old, Father William*; Lucy as the Fish-Footman, telling Alice that there was no use in knocking at the door because "I'm on the same side of the door as you are and secondly, because they're making such a noise inside, no one could possibly hear you." David as the Duchess, nursing a baby which turns into a pig; the Cheshire tiger; the mad parrot's tea party; the croquet party, and finally Alice returning up the tree again where she was at the beginning. I can't possibly include the whole of her play but I thought you would like to have a flavour of it. It's all on film anyway.

Everybody overacted appallingly and the audience enjoyed every minute. We took our bow amidst cheers and applause, and I pushed Alice to the front because she had written it all and produced it, so we all gave her an extra cheer. She had fulfilled her wish of a lifetime, even if she didn't expect it to happen quite like that on a tropical island.

We left everything where it was, because we were halfway through the jungle now and would be coming back this way to pick up the costumes. It was time to climb the hill for the last event of the day's programme.

Imagine if you can a pilgrimage of forty or so people emerging from the jungle into the sunlight, and gradually climbing up quite an easy slope over ground bare of any trees but just a few small bushes, hard earth, occasional rocky outcrops and scrubby grass. Everything was quiet apart from our puffing and panting. We didn't want to rush the adults, so we took it steadily with plenty of rests as well as opportunities to take in the views as they opened up every step of the way. This was going to be our last visit to the summit, so we wanted to savour every moment. There were no odd flutterings today, nor booming sounds, nor high chirrupings – where they had come from, and where they had gone, heaven only knows! – simply a serene atmosphere, with beautiful views of sea and sky, trees and beach. How sad that we have to leave! That was my thought, and probably others felt the same.

Soon the ground flattened out, and there she was up ahead: Polly the Lory, on the top of her pole! She looked no different from yesterday, none the worse for her night in the open air. If anything, she looked more resplendent than ever, her feathers fluttering in the breeze and glowing in the sunshine. Expressions of amazement and wonder came from our parents, and of course there was much clicking of mobiles as they sought to capture the scene. After a few minutes, everyone had made it to the top, and had gathered round our mascot. Now Christian had a quiet word with Zak, asking him to make an announcement about the singing. (I suspect Christian had had enough of being 'in charge' and giving all the orders, it had been a huge responsibility for him, after all.)

Zak nodded, and strumming his guitar announced to the assembled crowd, "So now we're going to have a little sing-song, everyone. You heard our anthems at the sports this morning, so hopefully you've picked 'em up okay and will all be able to join in this time. So if you'd all like to join hands and form a circle round Polly, let's give her a good final send-off."

It wasn't a bad little speech, and it had the desired effect. We sang each anthem twice, and by the second time all the adults had joined in, the dads giving them extra depth and volume, of course. The songs went with a swing, and we swayed with the beat as we danced around the pole. Then everyone collapsed in a heap with exhaustion, and we all drank masses from our water-bottles. We knew it would soon be time to go, but nobody wanted to. Instead small groups formed (and it was good that the adults mixed with us, and not just among themselves) and we had a time for chatting about the week, reflecting on everything that had happened, the highlights and lowlights, the discoveries and surprises.

Everything after this was banal and dreary: walking down the hill, gathering our stuff, walking to the ferry, leaving the island. In fact, it was all so sad that I cannot bring myself to write about it. So I am going to end the story there, on a perfect afternoon, with enough breeze for Oliver *at last* to fly his kite from the top of the hill and the sun sinking all too rapidly towards the western horizon, preparing to give us our final sunset of dazzling colourful wonder.

14
Some Explanations

I am delighted that the book has finally made it into print, and my first wish is to thank everyone who has made it possible, from Dr Crabb, our enlightened headmaster, to the teachers who took us, our parents who allowed us to go, the authorities on the main island who cooperated so brilliantly, the hotel, the ferrymen, my editor and publishers, my mum who proofread and polished up my English, and anyone else on the way who made even the smallest contribution.

I also want to thank my classmates who were so fantastic and in particular Christian who was prepared to take on the responsibility of being in charge of us. He was amazing, and we all love him to bits for what he did. As a group we really bonded over the week, and now I know that I have fifteen friends for life – who could ask for more than that?

When we returned to school for our final week, we worked on our projects: writing them up, drawing, painting, composing, whatever they needed. We managed to make a great big display of everything in the Assembly Hall, and on the very last evening of term David showed his film which he had been staying up late over the last few nights to complete. He had done a great editing job, even including some simple titles like 'Day One', 'Day Two' etc and 'Rehearsal for *Alice'* and 'Island Olympics', so he made it look very professional.

I don't think they really believed their eyes, and it even made us wonder if it had really happened like that. But just imagine a film of this book and now realise that this is what we experienced, so it must have been true. After the film, we gave a concert of the songs written by Zak, and the trio for 'cello, guitar and flute, and we also acted a few scenes from *Alice in Jungleland,* to show how we had spent our time, and how the island had inspired us.

In those final days, I also managed to catch up on my last remaining interviews for this book, including one with Dr Crabb and one with Mr Thompson, because I wanted some of the background to our trip. It was during this that Dr Crabb told me about that confrontation he'd had with Mrs Seymour. I thought this would be worth including so I wrote out my own version of it and then very sheepishly showed it to Mrs Seymour, asking her if she would allow me to include it in my novel, allowing for any modifications she might insist on. She roared with laughter when she read it, saying, "The interview didn't quite go like that! You've made me out to be a real battleaxe, haven't you? But it's fine; by all means include it if you want to, it's very funny!"

So then I was able to get to work. I had all of the summer holidays to put it together, and Christian gave me permission to include his log-book entries, which was good of him.

I kept in touch with Maia, Karen and Victoria for their illustrations. Olivia also sent me some lovely crayon pictures of fish, and Oliver sent me a magnificent map of the island, well, you will have seen all these while you have been reading the book, and I hope you have enjoyed them. Eventually I found six publishers who were prepared to receive unsolicited manuscripts, and I sent it off at the end of August – and waited...

After four weeks I received a positive reply.

"Dear Miss D...

We have enjoyed reading your book, *The Castaways,* and we would very much like to publish it..." and so on. I leapt for joy, informed everyone of the news, and wrote to the other five publishers as well.

And now, a year later, here is my book, in print! Unfortunately, we were not able to include a CD of all the music inside the back cover as we had hoped, nor any of the illustrations. But I'm sure my readers have active imaginations and maybe if the book goes into a second edition… Well, who knows?

I am hopeful about future editions because although *The Castaways* has not yet hit the shelves, as they say, we have already had so much advance publicity that I can't believe it won't be successful. The secret ingredient is that we are all so young! I am the firm's youngest-ever published author and even now they can't quite decide how to categorise my book: teenage, young adult, general fiction, non-fiction, travel adventure – a bit of everything, really. Well, I will leave that up to their marketing department. We have been promised a proper book launch, and there is even the possibility of some TV coverage, so I'm keeping my classmates closely in touch with everything that's going on. Sometime soon we will be having a reunion which will be great, because it's been over a year since we have all been together.

One thing we have absolutely sworn to as a group is not to disclose the identity and whereabouts of our island. Our lips are sealed on this point for obvious reasons and apart from anything else it adds a little mystique to our adventure which the publishers are delighted about.

Before I conclude, I need to tell you about my chat with David, our cameraman. I wanted to know his thoughts about the various strange incidents on the island. As I suspected, he had carefully catalogued each one, holding them up to the scrutiny of his rational judgement. So what were his findings, I asked him.

"I got absolutely nowhere," he answered with a smile.

"What do you mean, nowhere?"

"Well, let's put it like this: I had a number of different theories but I couldn't be sure about any of them and therefore I couldn't come to any conclusions which satisfied me."

"Oh, that's disappointing."

"Well, yes and no. Because it meant that I had to ask somebody else for their opinion. I'm only thirteen after all, so what do I know?"

"So who did you ask?"

"My dad, of course. He is the fount of all knowledge when I get stuck, and he is also a professional anthropologist so he knows a thing or two about primitive cultures and societies."

"But there wasn't any culture or society on that island," I pointed out.

"Exactly. And that's why, as he tried to explain to me, there were still some traces of its original spirit world, if you can believe that. You see, what he tried to explain to me was that ancient cultures, such as the ancient Egyptians and the Greeks (and a few others which I can't remember) were more closely in touch with the 'spirit of place', as he put it. You remember how we used to be told in classical mythology about dryads, nymphs and water sprites haunting groves, waterfalls and woodlands, and so on. While humans were still 'treading lightly on the earth' (again, those were his words – quite nice, I think), they could sort of commune with these spirits, apparently. Well, it's all in their literature anyway and he didn't think it was entirely made up or fanciful. But we're completely out of touch with it nowadays, basically because we've made such a heavy footprint upon the world that the dryads and nymphs have all fled, not surprisingly."

"Do you believe all this, David?"

"Well, I find it very interesting, let's put it like that, and I am also trying to be as open as possible to these ideas. Dad had hinted at some of these things before the trip, and he had told me to look out for any strange incidents, and so I had taken this on as my secret project: to look into and find evidence of any spirits on the island. I was totally sceptical, of course, but now I am not so sure."

"What was your dad's reaction when you told him about some of the funny goings-on?"

"He wasn't surprised in the least. He said it seemed to him that we had been given a mixed reception when we arrived on the island, some of it friendly (such as when Tom and Oliver had heard fluttering noises, then had immediately looked at their watches and noticed it was time for them to hurry back to camp or they would be late), some of it comical (as in the play rehearsal when Alice got stuck in a bog) then the rather romantic incident (Dad called it a 'prompting') when Karen seemed to fall out of love with Zak and into love with Corey."

"I can hardly believe I'm hearing you say this, David," I said.

"That's almost what I said to my dad, who basically is a deep down rationalist just like me. But then he quoted me a couple of lines from Shakespeare, from *Hamlet* in fact, which are apparently very famous:

There are more things in heaven and earth, Horatio,
Than are dreamt of in your philosophy,

Which basically means that we don't know all the answers, so always keep your mind open to all possibilities, especially ones which run counter to your usual way of thinking."

"It's certainly very interesting. What else did he have to say, if anything?"

"He was interested in Corey's javelins which didn't throw properly and then there was this curious sound which he heard. Now we all know what Corey's like: very enthusiastic and energetic but inclined to rush in like a bull in a china shop. He always reminds me of one of those Red Setter dogs which leap and charge around the place, full of fun and affection, but can go a bit wild. Dad suspected that Corey had been somewhat over-energetic in pulling down trees, and chopping away with his axe to make everything he needed such as javelins and hurdles; maybe there was some backlash for this. What was needed, Dad said, was for somebody to see what was going on, to tune in, as he put it, and so keep the peace, basically to be more respectful of the island and its primitive unspoiled nature, and then, by tuning in to the 'spirit of place', we wouldn't have any more trouble. Fortunately, we did have someone."

"Oh, you mean Christian?"

"No, it wasn't him, although he was very good, Dad said. But he added that it needed somebody rather more pagan, if you like, who was more in touch with the island's vibrations. I realised at once who he meant."

"Well, I don't."

"It was Zak."

"Zak?"

"Yes, our wandering minstrel. Dad had a chat with him on the mountaintop and realised that Zak had done more than anyone to appease the spirits, calm them down and bring them onto our side."

"Through his music, do you mean?"

"Exactly. You remember how he didn't like our class poem because it didn't carry the right sound or vibration for the island. So he adapted it and then it was more in harmony with the atmosphere. Dad said that music and song and harmony are really important ways of tuning into other cultures and places. It's like a universal language which can break down barriers between people and cultures, as well as places. This was him as an anthropologist talking from his experience, and then I began to believe that what he had told me might just possibly be true."

David paused. "But there's only one way we'll ever find out, isn't there?" he said after a moment.

"What's that?"

"We'll have to go back there, and continue our research."

"Wow, David! Do you think that'll ever happen?"

"I don't see why not, in five or ten years' time maybe. Wouldn't you like to?"

"Of course I would, and I'm sure all the others would too."

"Then you can write a sequel."

"*The Castaways Return*... hmm, I like the sound of that."

"Me too."